Cesare Pavese

Born Santo Stefano Belbo in a village in the province of Cuneo, Cesare Pavese (1908–1950) was educated in Turin, the city that became the setting and inspiration for much of his writing. After graduation he translated the works of a number of important British and American authors, introducing such major writers as James Joyce, Ernest Hemingway and Herman Melville to the Italian public; their work was also to have a profound effect on Pavese's own. During the 1930s he was a committed anti-fascist, for which he was arrested, imprisoned and placed in internal exile in a small village in southern Italy, an experience that provided the basis for *The Political Prisoner*. Upon his release he continued to associate himself with resistance movements, although he never took up arms. After the war Pavese found increasing literary success, winning the Strega prize in 1950. However, this coincided with spiralling depression, and, following the end of his relationship with the American actress Constance Dowling, he committed suicide in the summer of that year.

THE
POLITICAL PRISONER

CESARE PAVESE

THE
POLITICAL PRISONER

Translated from the Italian by W.J. Strachan
and with a foreword by Nick Johnstone

PETER OWEN
London and Chester Springs, PA, USA

PETER OWEN PUBLISHERS
73 Kenway Road, London SW5 0RE

Peter Owen books are distributed in the USA by Dufour Editions Inc.,
Chester Springs, PA 19425–0007

Translated from the Italian *Il Carcere*
First published in Great Britain by Peter Owen 1955
English translation © Peter Owen 1955
First Peter Owen Modern Classics edition 2008
Foreword © Nick Johnstone 2008

ISBN 978 0 7206 1262 2

A catalogue record for this book is available
from the British Library

Printed and bound in Great Britain by
CPI Bookmarque, Croydon, CR0 4TD

Foreword

Like so many people in awe of the writings of Italian author Cesare Pavese, I came to his work after reading Susan Sontag's essay about him, 'The Artist as Exemplary Sufferer', in her collection *Against Interpretation*. I was ripe for her recommendation, having recently returned from a short stay in Turin, the Italian city around which Pavese's life and death revolved. I was also in the middle of a full-blown obsession with the films of Michelangelo Antonioni and soon after learned, excitedly, that his 1955 film *Le Amiche* was an adaptation of Pavese's 1949 novel *Among Women Only*. For this reason, I read *Among Women Only* first, an atmospheric, slow-burning novel built upon a young woman's attempted suicide and the high probability of her trying again.

I loved how Pavese kept the story on a knife edge between sensuous and despairing, bleak and hopeful, banal and ecstatic. I loved his elliptical approach to narrative, his poet's ear for a mesmerizing sentence, the way he let the story wander, never made it run.* I loved that he wrote about this young woman's crumbling mind with the sensitivity and authenticity of one who had been there himself. And, of course, later I learned the novel was prophetic. At the end of *Among Women Only* the young woman, Rosetta, commits suicide, by taking an overdose in a Turin hotel room. The novel earned 42-year-old Pavese the prestigious Italian Strega prize for literature on 24 June 1950.

---

*Pavese's poetry is published by Carcanet (UK) and Copper Canyon Press (USA) in the collection *Disaffections: Complete Poems 1930–1950*.

But no accolade could help lift him up. On 27 August that same year he committed suicide, like Rosetta, by taking an overdose in the Hotel Roma e Rocca Cavour in Turin.

Next, I read *The Leather Jacket*, a collection of short stories characterized by yearning and isolation. After that, *The Devil in the Hills* (1948), a shimmering novel about three young men with too much time on their hands, meandering through a long, thrilling summer under the influence of a self-destructive alcoholic play-boy. By the time I read *The Moon and the Bonfire* (1950), a contemplative novel about a fortysomething Italian émigré returning, after a twenty-year exile in California, to the landscape of his childhood in rural Piedmont, I was hooked on Pavese's dolorous, sensuous tales of beautiful, tempting, flawed women – many of whom remind me of the characters Monica Vitti plays in the classic early Antonioni films *L'Avventura*, *L'Eclisse* and *Il Deserto Rosso* – and the listless, conflicted men who fall in love with them.

The fifth book I picked up was *The Political Prisoner* (1949), a short novel based on Pavese's May 1935 arrest for anti-fascist activities. After a brief spell of imprisonment, Pavese was sentenced to 'confinement' in Brancaleone, a remote coastal village in Calabria in the south of Italy. Although he was free to roam about the village, he had to report to the police station every day and was not allowed to send letters. As a direct result of this restriction of communication, on his release in May 1936 and his return to Turin he was devastated to find that the woman with whom he had been in love at the time of his arrest had married another man. His experiences in Brancaleone informed *The Political Prisoner* (1949), a novel preoccupied with the sea, claustrophobic small-village life, women both attainable and unattainable and the philosophical question of what it means to be imprisoned.

The novel opens with Stefano contemplating 'the invisible walls of his cell', reflecting on the simple locals, for whom 'the sea was the sea'. Like Pavese, Stefano must have his movements monitored, his presence noted by the local police. He swims, tentatively gets to know the villagers, fantasizes about Concia – a barefoot, dark-skinned servant girl who 'embodies all the wildness of the fields and the geranium flowers' – and alternately pursues or flees a covert sexual fling with an abandoned wife and mother, Elena, who is 'always clean and wholesome under her black dress and her white skin soft to the touch' and desperately hoping for a committed romantic partner. Stefano, however, sees Elena as one more element of his imprisonment:

> He had taken comfort in the illusion that his bedroom, Elena's body and the beach he walked on every day composed so minute and absurd a world that he had only to put his thumb in front of his eye to blot it all out.

In his gradual acceptance of the detention, which runs parallel to his deepening involvement with Elena and ever-more frequent sightings of Concia, Stefano begins to adjust to his insular but ill-defined new life. As reader, one feels the lack of boundaries in his imprisonment but also their cunning authority.

Late in the novel, as Stefano awaits a pardon, he simultaneously craves the pardon that will return him to life as he knew it and dreads it, because it will destroy this incredibly simple life of sleep, sea, Elena, Concia and reporting to the police. It's a remarkable novel, Pavese slowly revealing everybody in the story to be living in their own form of detention or imprisonment, imposed or self-imposed, everybody slave to something or someone: desire, ideals, government, lovers, parents, circumstance, geography, gossip, time.

The sixth Pavese book I read was another short novel, also included here, *The Beautiful Summer* (1949). Like *The Devil in the Hills* it tracks a group of listless young Italians, looking for fun and love, over the course of a summer. This time, however, Pavese writes of a group of young women. It's the story of Ginia, a sixteen-year-old employee at a dressmaker's shop, who, tiring of peers Rosa and Tina, falls under the spell of Amelia, a twenty-year-old 'dark, slim, devil-may-care' artist's model. As with Poli in *The Devil in the Hills*, Amelia's role here is that of a seductive, corrupting force. She insidiously undoes Ginia's youthful innocence, introducing her to painters, nude modelling, sexual experimentation and romantic despair. As the narrator warns, from the moment Ginia sets her sights on spending the summer in Amelia's shadow: 'One knew that Amelia, at any rate, was leading a different kind of life.' By the end of the novel, Amelia's radiance is dampened by illness and Ginia is privy to a knowingness she's not yet capable of dealing with, one that leads her to contemplate suicide. It's both a brutal coming-of-age novel and, like *The Political Prisoner*, pre-occupied with the exploration and testing of personal boundaries.

I've since gone on to read everything that Cesare Pavese wrote, and the same themes of yearning and isolation, love and lust, innocence and experience, joy and misery, fantasy and reality, passion and corruption weave throughout all his work. And the sad, horrible fact of his suicide is always there, too, lurking beyond the words, just as the idea of it was always lurking there *in* the words as he wrote them. Pavese knew it was his destiny to commit suicide. He willed it. The intention was set early in his adulthood. He lived, as the saying goes, like a scarecrow ever on the look-out for a bonfire on which to throw himself. In summer 1950, when the American actress Constance Dowling finished a two-year stint making films in Italy and returned to the USA, so breaking off her affair with Pavese, he found that bonfire. In his suicide note, he wrote: 'I forgive everyone and ask everyone's forgiveness. OK? Don't gossip too much.'

Far beyond the reach of that tragic scene in an anonymous hotel room, Pavese left behind some of the finest works in literature. Those works are safe from the bonfire. We will keep gossiping.

Nick Johnstone

ONE

Stefano knew that there was nothing unusual about the place, the inhabitants lived their daily lives, the earth produced; there, as on any other coast, the sea was the sea. Stefano felt happy by the sea; on first arriving he imagined it as the fourth wall of his prison, a huge wall of colour and coolness behind which he would be free to move about and forget the prison cell. From the very start he had filled his handkerchief with shells and pebbles. He had considered it a very human touch on the part of the *maresciallo** who examined his papers when the latter had replied to his request with the words, "Certainly, provided you can swim".

For some days Stefano contemplated the hedges of fig-trees and the faded horizon as if they were strange realities; that they composed the invisible walls of his cell was the most natural part about them. Stefano had accepted straight away and without demur this shutting-in of his horizon which imprisonment implied; for him who had just left a cell it represented freedom. Furthermore he had the feeling of this country-place around him, and the shy, inquisitive glances of the people seemed to him a guarantee of their friendliness. The arid fields, the vegetation, the sea with its changing moods, however, seemed strange to him at first. He could not take his eyes off them and they were continually in his mind. But as the memory of his real prison life faded even these presences receded into the background.

Maresciallo, an officer in the Carabinieri.

It was in fact on the sea-shore that Stefano was conscious of a different kind of depression one day when, having exchanged a few words with a youth who was drying himself in the sun, he had swum out to his daily rock which served as a buoy. "The villages are dirty here", the youth had said, "they all leave here for more civilised parts. Well, there it is! You and I have to stick here".

He was a dark-skinned, muscular young man, a *guardia di finanza* from Central Italy, on tax-collecting duties. He spoke in clear-cut tones which Stefano found attractive and they often met at the local inn.

Sitting on the rock with his chin resting on his knees, Stefano looked towards the desolate shore through half-closed eyes. The sun was beating down on it mercilessly. The *guardia di finanza* had compared his lot to his own, and Stefano's sudden distress arose from a sense of humiliation. The rock, the small stretches of water provided no real escape from the sea-shore. There was no solitude unless he could get away from those squat houses, those cautious people collected there between the sea and the mountain. Especially if — as Stefano suspected — the *guardia* had applied the term 'civilised' only out of politeness.

In the morning Stefano went through the village — the long street parallel to the sea-shore — and looked at the low roofs and the clear sky while the inhabitants eyed him from their doorsteps. Some of the houses had two floors, and the painted facades had been bleached by the sea air: an occasional piece of foliage behind a wall brought back memories. Between one house and the next he could catch a glimpse of the sea, and each of these gaps took Stefano by surprise like an unexpected friend. The gloomy, cave-like entrances under the low doors, the dark faces, the reserve of the women even when they came out into the street to empty their earthenware pots made a contrast with the bright atmosphere outside that increased Stefano's feeling of isolation. His stroll came to an end under the doorway of an inn where he went so that he could sit down and enjoy his freedom until it was warm enough for him to go and have his bathe.

At first Stefano passed many sleepless nights in his tumble-down house because it was at night that the strangeness of the day assailed him, causing a tingling in his blood. In the dark the murmur of the sea became a thundering roar, the cool breeze a high wind, the recollection of people's faces a torment. The whole of the nocturnal countryside seemed to hurl itself upon his extended body. When he woke up again the sun brought him peace.

Stefano would sit at his door in the sunlight, watching as it were for his liberty, as if he left his prison every morning. Sometimes customers entered the inn whom he found disturbing. At various times in the day the *maresciallo* of the carabinieri cycled past.

The motionless road, gradually making its way southward, strode past Stefano of its own accord; there was no need to follow it. He always had a book with him which he held in front of him and dipped into now and again.

It gave him pleasure to greet, and be greeted by familiar faces. The *guardia di finanza*, who was taking his coffee at the counter, gave him a courteous 'goodday'.

"You're a sedentary man", he said with a touch of

sarcasm, "whenever I see you, you are always sitting down either at table or on the rock. Your world doesn't extend very far!"

"True enough; my movements are limited too", replied Stefano, "and I come from a great distance away".

The *guardia* laughed. "They have told me about your case. The *maresciallo* is certainly a stickler but he realises the sort of person he is dealing with. He even lets you sit in the inn where you have no right to be".

Stefano was not always sure when the *guardia* was joking and he seemed to hear the uniform behind those clear accents.

A plumpish young man with vivacious eyes stopped at the door, listening to them. Suddenly he said, "Eh, yellow stripes, can't you see that the engineer is sorry for you and that you are boring him?" The *guardia* exchanged a smile with Stefano. "In that case you are irritation number three".

They all exchanged glances, mollified or amused as the case might be, but Stefano felt the joke was beyond him and tried to weigh and assess the glances they gave him. He realised that to break down the barrier he only needed to get to know the capricious laws governing this light-hearted banter and he could join in himself. Everybody in the place talked in this mocking way with a similar exchange of knowing looks. Other people with nothing special to do came in, and the game extended.

The plump youth, whose name was Gaetano Fenoaltea, was the expert at it, and as he lived directly opposite the inn in the shop which along with the other property round about, belonged to his father, he could stroll across without technically abandoning his work.

These idle folk were astonished that Stefano should go down to the sea-shore every day, though now and again some would walk there with him. They had even drawn his attention to the convenient rock. But they did so to keep him company or just for a whim. They could not understand his habit; it seemed childish to them. They could swim and were more familiar with the water than he, having played in it as boys, but for them the sea meant nothing or was merely somewhere where you could relax. The only one who spoke of it seriously was the young shopkeeper, who asked him whether he had ever spent seasons on the Riviera before the last 'show-down'. And although Stefano went out at dawn certain mornings and strolled alone along the wet sands to look at the sea, he himself began to dread the solitude when he heard at the restaurant that no one was coming down that day, and he would limit his time there to a bathe and an odd half-hour.

When they met in front of the inn, he and the plump youth would be content just to nod a greeting, for Gaetano preferred to show himself when a good company was gathered inside. On such occasions he was able, without any direct conversation with him and by joking with the others, to isolate Stefano in a sphere of reserve.

After a few days he became loquacious with him too. He took his arm affectionately and said, "Close your book, engineer, we don't have school here. You're on holiday. Show these lads the stuff you Northern Italians are made of".

This taking of his arm was always so unexpected that it reminded Stefano of the time when in his adolescent days, with beating heart, he had passed women in the street. He did not find it difficult to resist this effusiveness, especially as it embarrassed him in front of other people. During these early days Stefano had felt too much under the scrutiny of those glances to accept his friendliness in a natural way. But Gaetano's amiable expression was a guarantee of the others in the inn, and although he could eye you coldly when he wanted, his imperious manner had the artlessness that usually accompanies it.

It was therefore of him that Stefano inquired if there were any girls round about and, if so, why there were none to be seen on the beach. Slightly embarrassed, Gaetano explained that they bathed in a place set apart on the other side of the shore and when Stefano smiled derisively, he admitted that they did not often leave their houses.

"But there are some?" insisted Stefano.

"I should say!" replied Gaetano, beaming. "Our womenfolk grow old early in life but are all the prettier in their youth. They have a dazzling beauty that outshines the sun and disarms men's eyes. They are real ladies, our girls. That is why we keep them shut up".

"We don't have any of these hot glances where I come from!" said Stefano calmly.

"You have your work, we have love".

Stefano lacked the curiosity to go to the river to spy on the bathers. He accepted the tacit law of the segregation of the sexes as he accepted everything else. His life was bounded by imaginary walls of air. But he remained unconvinced that these lads made love. Possibly behind the permanently closed shutters of these houses some of the beds had a slight acquaintance with love and a few brides enjoyed their heyday. But not these boys. Stefano

12

had indeed surprised conversations about 'escapes' into the town — not invariably on the part of bachelors — and allusions to farm wenches, held in such contempt that you could discuss them openly.

This lack of female company depressed him most at dusk. He would relinquish his corner in the house and sit down on a heap of stones to watch the passers-by. The semi-darkness was illuminated by lights, shutters were flung open to the cool of the evening. There was a faint rustle and a sound of whispering as people went by, sometimes in chattering groups. There were also isolated bunches of more brightly dressed young women. They did not venture far and were soon on their way back again into the village.

There were no couples to be seen. When any of the groups passed each other, they exchanged cursory glances. Stefano liked this reserve; he was not allowed to leave his lodging after sundown and more than the rest of the inhabitants he favoured the night and the forgotten solitude of the darkness. So much indeed had he forgotten how gentle it was that a puff of wind, the sound of a footstep, the vast shadow of the mountain peak against the pale sky was enough to make him drop his cheek on his shoulder as if a friendly hand was caressing him. As the darkness cut off his horizon he was conscious of an enlarged field of freedom for his thoughts.

He was always alone at this time, and he also spent the larger part of the afternoon in solitude. They played cards at the inn during the afternoon and if Stefano joined in, he gradually grew restless and felt the urge to go out. Sometimes it would be as far as the sea-shore, but this bathing naked and alone in the green Mediterranean depressed him and caused him to dress hurriedly in the already chilling air.

He would then leave the village which seemed too small. The hovels, the hillside rocks, the leafy hedges once more turned into a lair of a sordid people with prying eyes and hostile smiles. He walked away from the village along the wide road which led through olive groves to meadows bordering the sea. He strode along purposefully, wishing the time away, hoping something might happen. Seeing the level horizon stretch before him, he felt as if he must walk on to infinity. The village disappeared behind the hill, and the surrounding mountains rose and interrupted the skyline.

Stefano did not go far. The road was virtually a raised terrace which allowed a view of the desolate seashore and the empty countryside. In the distance where the road turned, there were signs of green foliage, but half-way along Stefano stopped and looked all round him. Everything was grey and unfriendly between the air above him and the distant hills. Now and again he would catch sight of a peasant in the fields or he would see a figure crouching below the terrace-road. Stefano who had been walking along with bitterness in his heart, then felt a peace that was almost painful, a kind of mournful sadness, and slowly he retraced his footsteps home.

On his way back to the village he was almost happy. The outlying houses had a friendly look about them. There they were snug under the hill, warm in the clear air, and the knowledge that the sea stretched peacefully before them lent them almost the same attraction they had had on the day of his arrival.

At the entrance to the village, among the first houses,

stood one apart from the rest between the street and the sea-front. Stefano made a habit of glancing at it every time he passed by. It had grey stone walls and an outside staircase that led to a small loggia at the side opening on to the sea. Where the windows coincided — though they were usually closed — the onlooker from the road got the impression that the building was perforated and filled with sea. The luminous panel stood out clear and intense like a patch of sky seen from a prison window. There were some scarlet geraniums on the window-sill. Stefano always stopped to have a look.

His heart gave a leap one morning when he saw a girl on the stairway. He had seen her before walking along in the village — the only girl in point of fact — she stepped in a sprightly, almost cheeky dance, raising her brown, goatlike face with each upward swing of her hip. Her confidence amused him. She was evidently a servant, for she went about barefoot and carried water sometimes.

Stefano had an idea that the women of the place were white-skinned and plump, like the flesh of a pear, and so this encounter surprised him. He allowed his imagination to play with the young woman in the seclusion of his ramshackle house, conscious of a sense of freedom and detachment, for the strange nature of the person in question liberated him from every pang of desire. The existence of a relationship between the geranium-filled window and the girl increased and enriched the play of his fancy.

Stefano spent the hottest hours of the afternoon stretched out on his bed, half-naked in the summer heat, and the white dazzle from the sun caused him to keep

15

his eyes almost closed. In the uneasy and murmuring stillness he felt alive and watchful, and sometimes he laid his hand on his hip. The girl's hips would be like that, slender yet strong.

Outside, beyond the iron railings, hidden by an embankment, was the Mediterranean. There occurred moments when the burning silence frightened him. Then he would shake himself and leap down from the bed in his underpants. He had reacted in the same way during the now remote days when he was in prison. From roof to terrace the bedroom had become a Turkish bath and Stefano moved over to the low window where the wall cast a little shadow and the earthenware pitcher stood to cool. Stefano stroked its damp, slender side, and raising it from the ground, applied it to his lips. With the water came an earthy taste that felt harsh against his teeth; he enjoyed this more than the water; it seemed to be the taste of the vessel itself. It suggested something wild and goatlike and yet smooth. It was all somehow mixed up in his mind with the colour of the geraniums.

Like everybody else in the place, the barefoot girl went to draw water in a similar vessel. She walked along with the rim resting obliquely on her hip, putting her weight on her ankles. All these vessels were smooth and elongated in shape; their colour was midway between brown and flesh-pink, some were paler. Stefano's was rose-tinted like a flushed cheek. Stefano was grateful to his landlady if only for this amphora. She was a stout, elderly woman who moved round with some difficulty. She sat in her tiny shop in the street, occasionally sending a boy over to take him water. Sometimes she sent him merely for the purpose of cleaning

16

his room. They swept it out, arranged his bed and did some washing for him. All this took place in the mornings when Stefano was out.

The joy of having a door to open and close once more, everyday objects, a table and a pen — things that made up the pleasure of his liberty — had lasted him a long time, like a convalescence, with the feeling of humility that accompanies it. Stefano was soon conscious of its precariousness as the discoveries became part of his habits.

A carabiniere would call round in the evening on rare occasions to make sure he was inside the house. After dusk and before dawn Stefano was not supposed to leave the building. The carabiniere would stop abruptly at the door, in the halo of light, nod a salute and go off. A companion waited for him in the shadow with his carbine slung over his shoulder. On one occasion the *maresciallo,* complete in cloak and top-boots, arrived. He was passing through on patrol. He had a word with Stefano on the doorstep and darted an amused glance at the interior of the room. Stefano was ashamed of all the rubbish piled up in the corner, the boxes, the general untidiness and the unsavoury smell as he thought of the spacious barracks on the little piazza which a carabiniere swept out each day, and the balconies overlooking the sea.

On the ground-floor of the barracks stood the cells with windows blocked in such a way that daylight could only filter in from above. Every morning as Stefano trod quietly by, he thought that, as far as dirt was concerned, these cells must be rather like his own room. Sometimes the sound of a voice would emerge or the rattle of a mess-tin, and then Stefano would know that

17

someone — peasant, thief or tramp — was imprisoned in the darkness within.

TWO

No one makes a home of a prison-cell, and Stefano never forgot the invisible walls round him. As he played cards in the tavern surrounded by the cheerful or tense faces of the other men, he sometimes saw himself alone and precarious, wistful at the thought of the invisible wall separating him from these casual acquaintances. But the *maresciallo*, who was prepared to turn a blind eye and made no objection to his visiting the tavern, was oblivious of the fact that at every memory, at every discomfort, Stefano repeated to himself that this was not his life, that these people and their good-humoured gibes were as remote from him as a desert and that he was a prisoner who one day would find his way home.

Gaetano greeted him every morning in a sly manner. Those knowing glances and that comic mouth became suddenly animated as he caught sight of Stefano. Gaetano preferred chatting to Stefano, with all of them hanging so to speak on their lips, to joining in the game. Two years previously Gaetano had been in Northern Italy as a sergeant.

The others were dry, dark-skinned men, ready to be interested and smile their approval if Stefano also spoke in a jocular vein. There was one, bald despite his youth, who would spread the newspaper out in front of him, run his eye from top to bottom of the long columns, glance at the onlookers and talk away in a quiet voice. A little girl that belonged to him arrived every now and

18

again with messages for him from his wife, who stood behind the counter of her little drug-store. The father snapped out some reply and the child would run off; Stefano, who listened in surprise the first few times, felt himself being stared at by the bald-headed man. The latter wore an apologetic smile, but like the smiles of all these people, even bald Vincenzo's was discreet and inoffensive; he did his best to avoid those dark, friendly eyes. There was a good deal of joking about Vincenzo's business. They asked him if he had learned to make his wife work while he was in Algeria. To which Vincenzo retorted that ordinary counter-work could be done perfectly well by a woman; women got on best with one another.

"At any rate you fill the shop with handsome errand-girls", said Gaetano, winking at Stefano. "As they do in other places, eh?"

"All depends on what you're selling", replied Vincenzo without raising his eyes.

There was a young man with a curly beard, sitting in a corner who sometimes chatted with the *guardia di finanza*. So far he had never greeted Stefano and he would leave the inn as he had come, without allowing Gaetano time to indulge in any chaffing. Stefano could not be certain but he had the impression that it was the same person who from astride his chair in front of the barber's saloon had been gazing on to the deserted piazza beneath the hot sun, the afternoon when he had emerged from the station handcuffed and burdened with a suitcase and had been escorted into the Town Hall by the carabinieri. Stefano found it impossible to form a very clear impression of his first arrival; his desperate fatigue, the sultry sea-air, his numbed arms, the bored,

19

disillusioned glances he had given the people, all mixed up with the new sights, formed a dazzling confusion in his brain. Then he had suddenly turned round, in search of the sea, the rocks, the vegetation and the streets; and he did not succeed in fixing the faces that had watched him as he crossed the piazza. At one time he felt that everyone had been indifferent to him and the place almost deserted; at another, that like a fair-crowd, lots of them had collected together and turned in his direction as he went by. It had been a Sunday, and he knew now that many idlers waited on Sunday mornings to see that train in.

The youth in question was called Giannino and he seemed hostile. Then one day with his back propped up against the counter, he lit a cigarette and addressed Vincenzo.

"What's the paper got to say? Have the Algerians used up all your soap yet? Have they eaten it like butter on bread?"

"It's all right for you to joke, Don Giannino, but if I was your age, I would go back there. It's an Eldorado, white Algiers" — and Vincenzo kissed his finger tips.

"Why 'white' when they're all black there? Has he given it a bath?" said Giannino, jerking himself away from the counter and going to the door.

"Vincenzo will return to Algeria when you return to San Leo, Giannino", said Gaetano.

Giannino smiled pleasantly. "Better to be chased after by women than have no money. The more women know you the more they track you down. Just like policemen!" Giannino laughed, compressing his lips, and went off.

A few minutes later Stefano followed him into the

street. He was setting off for the Town Hall to wind up the afternoon and collect his mail when Giannino darted out from a street.

"A word with you, engineer".

Stefano stopped, surprised.

"I need your expert advice. Do you know anything about houses? My father has designed a small villa and has forgotten about the stairs. Can you read plans?"

"I'm an electrical engineer of barely one year's standing", said Stefano, smiling.

"Oh, come, you know, I'm sure. Come to our place; you can advise us about lighting. What about this evening?"

"I can't manage tonight", Stefano smiled again.

"Yes, the *maresciallo* is a pal of mine. Do come . . .".

"Better not. You come to me".

All that evening Giannino had a ready and ingratiating smile, there in the half-light of the court-yard. There was no need for any light to see the white gleam of his teeth or to hear his courteous voice. He had sat down astride the chair, and against the aura of light from the door he merged into the darkness, and his voice mingled with the swish and the thud of the waves.

"It is too hot in the room and there's a smell", said Stefano. "I've kept up my prison habits. It's impossible to get fond of a cell. You can't make a room out of it".

"This light from above must hurt your eyes; it's too harsh. A candle would be better".

In the room, standing on a chest, could be seen a suitcase, as yet unpacked.

"Always ready to go off, I suppose?" Giannino had remarked from the door.

"It's there to ward off the evil spirits! The order for my transfer might arrive tomorrow, any day. One can't rest still even in bed; being a prisoner or internee is not a matter of being locked up; it is being dependent on a scrap of paper".

They looked at each other as they sat face to face. The sea splashed. Stefano smiled.

"At home, you folk have the reputation for being dirty but I think I am dirtier than you".

Giannino laughed, then suddenly became serious.

"We *are* dirty", he said. "But I get you, engineer. You keep your case packed ready for the same reason. We are a restless lot, contented everywhere else in the world except in our native place".

"It's not a bad hole".

"I'll believe that when you've unpacked your case", said Giannino, leaning his cheek on his arm.

Giannino's house also gave on to the sea, but Stefano went along to it the next day with some reluctance, having woken up in the grip of his usual anxiety. He invariably woke at dawn, worried, and lay on his bed with his eyes half-closed, postponing the moment when he should regain full consciousness. But the pleasure of drowsing was not for him; daylight and the sea called him, the room grew bright; and still floating among the shreds of his dreams, his heart ached with physical anguish. Leaping out of bed woke him up properly. That morning, however, his feeling of distress lasted until he gained the street; the peace of the previous night had evaporated as he remembered having talked too much about himself.

Giannino was not in. His mother, who knew nothing about Stefano, came and showed him into a room full

22

of dusty papers. The floor was of red tiles. The walls were as solid as rock. Through a tiny window he could see a little green foliage. Giannino had gone off at dawn. The mother's lips puckered into a smile when she heard his scheme.

Then the father entered; a wiry man with a luxuriant, tobacco-stained moustache which belied his seventy years. He knew about Stefano but he dismissed his scheme with a sweep of his hand. "I'd like you to talk it over with my son", he said. "I've already done my part".

"I'm afraid I shan't be much use to you", said Stefano. Giannino's father extended his arms, and his moustache curved up in a gesture of kindly gratitude.

The mother, who was a big woman, with a massive face, went to make the coffee. She poured it from a silver pot into tiny gilded cups, set out on the table without a tray. Father Catalano meanwhile, who had been laughing at her, began to stride up and down in front of the cracked wall and finally sat down.

Stefano was the only one who drank the coffee. The other two cups stayed half-empty on the table.

"I know all about your case, engineer", said the old man, his hands resting on his knees. "You are not the only one. I know what times we live in".

"How do you like it here?" asked the mother.

"How do you think", the old man flashed out. "Foul hole! Can't you get a job?"

Stefano stared at the photographs that stood on the various pieces of furniture, he gazed down on the faded rugs, and gave a non-committal reply. The stone-like chill in this old parlour was creeping up his legs. He refused a second cup of coffee, and the signora left them.

23

"I hope you will have a good influence on my rogue of a son", said the old man suddenly. He glanced round, smiling in an absent-minded sort of way, and when Stefano rose to say good-bye, he extended both arms. "We have felt honoured by your visit, engineer. Come again".

Stefano went home for a short time to collect a book. It was late morning and he could not get that chilly drawing-room with its chipped plaster walls out of his mind. He strained after a thought that he was certain had come to him a few moments earlier in that room and now became clearer: the barefoot maid with the swaying hips who belonged to the house with the geraniums must live in rooms like that and slide her feet over the red tiles. Or perhaps the grey house was of more recent date. But the gilded cups, dusty old knick-knacks, rugs and furniture, exhaled the spirit of a past age in the stone-cold atmosphere. One of those houses with its doors and windows perpetually shut which, perhaps once sunny and hospitable, had known a different life, a different warmth. To Stefano they were the villas of his childhood days, closed and deserted in the land of memory. The red, barren soil, the greyness of the olive-trees, the fleshy fig-tree hedges had once enriched these houses, now dead and silent except for a lithe, dark-skinned woman who seemed to embody all the wildness of the fields and the geranium flowers.

Stefano came across the daughter, no longer young, of the mistress of the house in the courtyard. She was gravely sweeping a heap of refuse into the ditch. He saw some of the children of the neighbourhood running about and playing on the roof-terrace, which was odd for that time of day. The woman smiled at him wanly, through all the clamour, as she always did when she met him.

Her face was puffy and pale and she was dressed in a respectable black dress. She was either a widow or separated from her husband who had packed her off to live in some distant place; even with these children she did not speak in the local dialect. She followed him up to the door of the room that had been done out, and Stefano felt he must turn round and thank her.

The woman stood still and put down her broom, unable to take her eyes off him. The bed now shaken up and re-made, gave an air of respectability to the whole room.

"One day you will go away", she said in her deep voice. "Will you remember us?"

Stefano saw a dish of Indian figs on the table. He tried to look reassuring and mumbled some sort of reply.

"We scarcely ever see you", said the woman.

"I'm looking for a book".

"You read too much because you're alone", she added, not moving.

She was always like this in the afternoons when she came to bring him something. Long silences ensued filled with glances from her, and Stefano felt both gratified and embarrassed. The woman blushed at her own obstinacy; her husky voice fell silent, as she yearned for a kind word. Stefano looked on, troubled.

"No; I am not alone", he said that morning in a loud voice, strode up to the door and, cupping her cheeks between his hands, drew them close to his face. He kissed her on the nape of her neck. The rushing feet of the boys could be heard pounding over the roof. This combination of embarrassment and boldness caused him to hug her to his breast. The woman did not try to get away; she clung to his body, but without allowing herself to be kissed.

Those irresistible mornings awoke a sudden physical desire in Stefano. The woman began to stroke his hair as if he were her child. Stefano did not know what to say. When he touched her breasts, she turned away, then looked at him with a grave smile.

Her face was flushed and tearful. She was almost handsome. She began to whisper, "No, not now. If you really care for me, I will come again. We must be careful. They have all got their eyes on us. I am as much alone as you are . . . No; if you love me, Vincenzino will be coming back. . . . Leave me now".

Vincenzino, a dark-skinned boy, did in fact return with the pitcher filled with water. Stefano helped him to put it down on the window-sill and fumbled for a coin. But Elena took her small nephew by the hand and led him out without turning round.

Stefano threw himself on the bed, smiling to himself. He imagined he could still see Elena's eyes staring at him. Again he felt a physical desire surge up inside him and he leaped down off the bed. It amused him finding himself in this situation at this unusual time of day; there was nothing he might not dare. He went out and along the beach so as not to meet her.

The sea, which he saw only as a background to his thoughts, was as lovely as it had been during his first days there. The little waves rippled at his feet with edges of foam. The smooth sand shone like marble. As Stefano made his way up towards the houses by the dusty hedge, his thoughts went back to the barefoot maid of the geraniums and he wished he could have embraced and kissed her instead of Elena. "It would be wonderful to meet her", he murmured aloud for the pleasure of hearing his own excitement. "Today is the day of deeds". He pictured her gay and dancing, dull-witted under that low forehead, wildly in love with him. He trembled as he imagined the mottled flesh of her breasts.

When he got to the inn, he found Vincenzo reading the newspaper. They exchanged greetings.

"Today seems like Sunday", remarked Stefano.

"Having your bathe, engineer? It's always Sunday for you!" Stefano sat down and mopped his brow. "Will you have a coffee, Vincenzo?"

Vincenzo folded up the newspaper and raised his head. His bald head wrinkled in a silly smile.

"Thank you, engineer".

His hairless crown looked like a baby's. Though he was still young, if he had a fit of the sulks, he was distressing to look at. The sort of head for a red fez.

"Always Sunday!" exclaimed Stefano. "You who have lived in the big town, must know how boring Sunday is".

"But I was young in those days".

"You're old now, I suppose!"

Vincenzo frowned. "One is old when one returns to one's native village. My life was lived elsewhere".

The coffee arrived and they sipped it quietly.

"What will you have to eat today, engineer?" Vincenzo suddenly asked as he caught sight of the hostess disappearing.

"A dish of *pasta*".

"Followed by some fried fish", said Vincenzo. "They

were selling rock salmon this morning, caught by moon-light. My mother bought some. It's scaly but good".

"Don't you see that it is not Sunday for me. The *pasta* will do me".

"Nothing else? Dammit, you're young still! You're not in the cells here".

"I have still one foot in. I don't get the allowance yet".

"The devil, but you ought to! They will certainly give it to you".

"I don't doubt it; meantime I eat olives".

"Why do you ruin yourself on coffees?"

"Isn't that what your Arab friends do? A coffee is cheaper than a dinner".

"I don't like it, engineer. *Pasta* and olives! It shall be on me".

"But, excuse me, I eat olives in the evening. They taste good with bread".

Vincenzo was flushed and put out. He folded his newspaper and flourished it. "So that's the extent of your earnings. Sorry, engineer, but you were mad. You can't argue with the government".

Stefano looked at him with expressionless eyes. Assuming this air of indifference helped to restore his peace of mind, it was like bracing one's muscles to receive a blow. But Vincenzo fell silent, and as his efforts met no resistance, Stefano began to smile. His smile was a real smile that morning though his lips were distorted. He had worn it when he looked at the sea, an automatic reaction but warm and unexpected.

That day Stefano did not eat at the inn. He took a parcel of bread home with him, avoiding the shop Elena's mother kept and glancing in Giannino's window; he hoped he would not have to spend the afternoon in solitude.

But no one came, and when he had eaten a lump of meat and a piece of bread dipped in oil, he threw himself down on his bed, resolved not to wake up until they tapped him on the arm.

He was restless, however, in the burning silence and he kept getting down for a drink, as he had done in prison, although he was not thirsty. This voluntary prison was worse than the other. Gradually Stefano began to hate himself because he lacked the courage to go right away from the place.

Later in the day he went to have the bathe he had neglected to have that morning, and the calm sunset waters soothed him a little, roasting his skin already tanned by the sun. He noticed Giannino Catalano waving his arms on the beach.

When he had got dressed again, they sat down together on the sand. Giannino had just got off the train; he had been in the town. He had caught sight of him going down to the seashore from the carriage window.

Stefano related with a smile what had taken place that morning at his friend's house.

"Oh, they will have explained to you that I am a ne'er-do-well", said Giannino. "They've thought of nothing else ever since I left school and acquired this beard".

Stefano quietly scrutinised his friend's bony face and his unkempt beard. In the cool, tranquil light, he seemed once more on the point of retrieving the memory he had of him sitting astride a chair, looking bored, that distant Sunday. Giannino pulled a small pipe out of his pocket.

"I've served in the army and seen a bit of the world", he remarked, thrusting his finger into the bowl. "Then I chucked it because it was too much like school".

"And what are you doing now?"

"What you are doing. Passing the time. And I keep an eye on my father to see his bricklayers don't do him down".

"Your father keeps an eye on you, more like", Stefano remarked.

"There's always someone keeping an eye on all of us", said Giannino, winking. "Such is life".

As he was lighting his pipe, the blue smoke curled up against the background of sea. Stefano followed it with his eyes and Giannino's words reached him, faintly.

"We are poor idiots. The small amount of freedom the government allows us, we let women snatch away from us".

"Better it should be the women", laughed Stefano. Giannino's voice assumed a serious tone.

"Have you found one yet?"

"What?"

"A . . . woman, dammit! "

Stefano looked at him jokingly.

"It is not easy here. And then it's against the regulations. 'Do not consort with women for the purpose of intimacy or for any other reason . . .' ".

Giannino leaped to his feet. Stefano followed him quickly with his eyes. "You are joking, engineer. You can keep a woman, surely?"

"I can get married, I suppose".

"Oh, then you'd just be a tame fiancé".

Stefano smiled. Giannino was calm now and made a move to sit down. The blue smoke curled past and floated towards the horizon, almost creating the illusion that it was from a passing steamer.

"Do any ever pass here?" asked Stefano, pointing out to sea.

"We are off any trade routes", replied Giannino. "Even when ships go by, they give us a wide berth. There's a hidden reef out there. I am even amazed that trains call!"

"It's a frightening thing in the middle of the night, the train", said Stefano. "I hear it whistle in my sleep. No one thinks of it in the daytime but at night it is as if it were splitting the terrace in two as it thunders across the deserted countryside in a panic to escape. It is like hearing the clang of the trams from inside the prison. One is thankful when morning comes".

"What you want is someone sleeping next to you", said Giannino softly.

"That would be 'intimacy' ".

"Rot", replied Giannino. "The *maresciallo* has two. It's every man's right".

" 'We have our work and you have your love-making', Don Gaetano Fenoaltea used to say to me".

"Fenoaltea? He's a fool. He wastes all his father's money on tarts. He has even put a thirteen-year-old servant in the family way".

Stefano's lips formed themselves into a smile and he rose to his feet with the pale sea behind him. His smile expressed disillusionment, for, on his first arrival he had believed in the innocence of this country village; but this belief was merely his reluctance to hear about the sordid acts committed by others. It was the light-hearted tone of the narrator rather than the particular incident that disgusted him. It stopped him regarding the bodies of

31

other people as simple objects for his amorous attentions. Before he left him, Giannino noticed this strained attitude and said no more. They parted at the inn door.

When he got back that evening, Stefano felt sure of himself. He found his pyjama jacket folded ready for him on his bed.

After dark, when the cobbler in the yard had put out his light, Elena appeared at his door and closed it behind her. Then she put the shutters to and leaned against them; she was dressed in black as if in mourning. She allowed him to embrace and kiss her, whispering to him to be silent.

The eyes in her frightened face were moist with tears. He realised he would not need to say anything, and he drew her up close to him. The air in the closed, brightly lit room was stifling.

THREE

Stefano got out of bed and went to the window. The woman, sitting in bed, her hands covering her breasts, gave a husky cry.

"What is it?" murmured Stefano.

"Don't open! They will see us".

Her hair was loose and beads of perspiration stood on her lips. She was slipping her clothes on in a panic, dashing towards the wall. Her pale legs showed up against her black skirt.

"Now can I open?" stammered Stefano.

Elena walked towards him, her forefinger pressed against her lips. Her eyelids fluttered imploringly. She gave him a somewhat petulant smile and laid her hand on his bare chest.

"I am going", she said gently.

"Stay a little while longer. It is so long since I kissed a woman". Elena smiled. "Yes, plead with me like that: I love it. You didn't press me like that before". Then large tears welled in her eyes and she took one of his hands and held it against her breast. While she lay there weeping in Stefano's arms, she gasped out, "Please go on talking like that. I love it when you talk. I am a woman, yes, a woman. I am your little mother".

The black material over her soft breast got in Stefano's way. He said gently, "We can go down to the sea-shore sometimes".

Elena's eyes drank up his words. "No; not on the shore. Do you really care about me? I am so afraid it is only my body you are after. Is that all you want?"

"I do care for you but I cannot deny that I desire your body".

Elena snuggled her face against his chest. "Get dressed, engineer, I am going off now".

Stefano slept heavily and woke up in the chill of the dawn, glad to be alone. As he prepared to go out, he reflected that next time he would have the lights out so that he would not have to smile, and he could imagine it was the young, barefoot girl beside him in the bed. "As long as she doesn't fall in love with me and blurt it out in the village".

During the subsequent days, Stefano only saw Elena once, when he startled her with tales about the *maresciallo's* visit on his rounds, but each time he went back to his room, he found there evidence of her modest yet bold presence. The bed was always re-made, the water supply renewed, and his handkerchiefs washed. He even found an embossed paper doily on the table.

Elena was glad he put the light out and in her ignorance as to what to do, clung to Stefano's breast; everything became very simple and there was no need to say anything. Stefano knew that Elena saw him passing in front of the shop, but he never entered; he would have felt embarrassed before her mother. There was one thing about Elena which distinguished her from the other women of the place; just as she differed from them in not speaking the local dialect, she differed too in that she was always clean and wholesome under her black dress and her white skin was soft to the touch. It made Stefano think of the days when she had lived in Liguria, as the wife of a soldier who had then deserted her.

"You will go away, too", she said to him in the dark. "You don't like it here and you will go away".

"Yes, perhaps to prison once more".

"Don't say such things; it brings bad luck; they happen if you do".

"Well, I keep my bag packed ready. How can you be sure of tomorrow?"

"No; you will return to your home and leave me".

Stefano spent a good deal of time, those days, sitting in the inn, and seldom strolled along the beach or the avenue of olive-trees which plunged down to the foot of the hill. He was exhausted, and as soon as he had swum to the usual rock, he lay there relaxed and contented under the clear sky and felt the beads of sweat trickle over his now firm, sun-tanned flesh. He continued to stare at the shore covered with the small huts, pink and buff under the shimmering sun and, rising high above the hill with its white summit, the old part of the village. Even his loneliness had changed its nature; he seemed to have absorbed those invisible walls into his body. Even his fatigue was not unpleasant, and some mornings, as he dried his lean body on the shore, he was overcome with a fit of wild hilarity, which expressed itself in subdued shouts.

The whole country and the life there seemed a kind of game to him, of which he knew the rules and could follow the progress without actually participating, master as he was of himself and his strange lot. The very torment of his loneliness added colour to his life. When he went up to the Town Hall to collect his mail, he did so with an impassive face, and the secretary who handed him a franked envelope, could not — with that piece of paper — fling open to him the magic portals of fantasy and bring him back into contact with a remote and far-off existence which he would have now deemed impenetrable if he had not recognised himself as once belonging to it. The dismayed face of the lively secretary showed a fresh astonishment on each occasion.

"You don't need to call every day, engineer. We know you have no intention of escaping".

The secretary made an expressive gesture, opening wide his dark-ringed eyes.

"Can you send my post to the house then?" asked Stefano.

The secretary opened the palms of his hands as a sign of hopelessness.

On the little stony road between the church and the Town Hall Stefano not infrequently met the *maresciallo*. Stepping aside, he would salute him, and sometimes they would stop and chat. Dark, sunburnt peasants went by, wearing white stockings, doffed their berets and looked down on the ground. Stefano nodded back in return. The *maresciallo's* curly head was turned rigidly in the direction of the sea.

"So you do not intend to do any gardening?" he said after a long silence.

Stefano shook his head.

". . . These peach-trees are dying on me".

"You have plenty of them".

The *maresciallo* glanced all round him. "The whole of the espalier behind the barracks. The prisoner whose advice I got about them, has been committed for punishment. I hear you accompany Giannino Catalano on his expeditions. I suppose you can shoot then?"

"No", replied Stefano.

The presence of Giannino helped him not to feel he was Elena's slave, and gave a meaning to all the waiting about he did in the inn and in idle chat with the others. He left the house with the knowledge that these streets concealed all manner of surprises, differences of opinion and sympathies which gave the place a more concrete reality and a more definite potentiality. So the less important people receded into the background as the sea and landscape had after his first days there. But Stefano very quickly realised that the game that life there had become, could vanish like the illusion it was.

Gaetano Fenoaltea had eyed Giannino's relationship with Stefano with suspicion, and he evidently saw that something was afoot about which he was being kept in the dark. . . . Stefano was convinced of it the next day when he went up with him to the 'old village'.

Gaetano had linked arms with him and told him it was the *festa* of the Madonna of September and that the *maresciallo* had said he could take him along. "The whole place goes up there and you can come with me. You'll see some pretty women up there".

The hill was a veritable mount of olives, barren and burnt. On arriving at the summit, Stefano had looked at the sea and the distant houses. During the whole excursion he had taken comfort in the illusion that his bedroom, Elena's body and the beach he walked on every day composed so minute and absurd a world that he had only to put his thumb in front of his eye to blot it all out. And yet that strange world, seen from an even stranger place, continued to be part of him.

Next day, as he sat smoking a cigarette, Stefano felt he was enjoying the unaccustomed fatigue resulting from his mountain-descent of the previous night, and he had an agreeable sense of heaviness in all his limbs. It had been such an age since he had walked across country under the stars. At that hour the whole mountain had been crawling with cheerful groups of people who recognised each other by their voices, cried out and stumbled into the bushes in the dark. He could hear women laughing and chattering behind and before them on their way down. Someone was trying to start up a song. At intervals they would stop and move over into different groups.

Vincenzo, Gaetano and the others making up the company were now in the inn. They were joking about the *guardia di finanza* who, unaccustomed to the wine, had made a beast of himself and was perhaps even then lying in a ditch, asleep.

"You are a strait-laced lot", remarked Stefano. "Where I come from they all get tight".

"Have you enjoyed yourself, engineer?" asked one man in a loud voice.

"He's not enjoyed himself because he has no use for women", said Gaetano.

Stefano smiled. "Women? I didn't see any. Unless by 'women' you mean those pieces of skirt who were dancing among themselves under the eyes of the parish priest. Don't they ever dance with men?"

"It wasn't supposed to be a wedding feast", replied Gaetano.

"Didn't you find any kindred soul?" asked bald-headed Vincenzo.

"Yes — let's hear, who was the best-looker?" exclaimed Gaetano, interested.

They all looked at Stefano. Their deep-set and malicious eyes gleamed with anticipation. Stefano turned away and threw down his cigarette-end.

"Look here, I've no wish to start any knife-throwing", he said quietly, with a polite nod, "but in my opinion the best-looking woman was not there. You have a real beauty but she was not there . . .".

He had not intended to speak and there he was letting go. The others' excitement lent him an importance that compelled him to go on. He felt himself one of them and that he was sharing their foolishness. He smiled.

"She was not there . . .".

"But who is she?"

"I don't know. Speaking frankly I think she's a servant girl. She is as handsome as a goat. Something between a statue and a goat".

Under the pressure of questions he took refuge in silence. They mentioned various names. He replied that he knew nothing about it. But from the descriptions

38

they gave, he gathered that she was called Concia. If it were she, they told him, she came from the mountains and was a real mountain-goat, ready for any caprice. But they could not see where her beauty came in.

"You don't seem to like them when they are fully grown women!" remarked Vincenzo, and they all burst out laughing.

"But Concia did go to the *festa*", said a dark young man. "I saw her wandering behind the church with two or three young lads. Your fine beauty is a baby-snatcher!"

"Who else would want her? She has 'served' old Spano, who kept her as a servant", said Gaetano, eyeing Stefano.

Stefano dropped the topic. Once more he felt a twinge of that physical loneliness that had never left him all day amid the festive throng and the strange sky above him. The whole day Stefano had been isolated as if outside time itself, pausing to gaze at the narrow streets open to the sky. That was why Giannino had chaffed him, saying, "Come on, go with Fenoaltea. You'll find it amusing".

Stefano would have liked to mingle with the rest of them and forget the clear afternoon outside, singing and shouting in that room with its low wooden ceiling where the jars of wine were standing on the window-sills to cool. That was what Pierino, the *guardia di finanza*, had done. Or, emboldened by the wine — which could also be his excuse -- he might have sought out Concia in that motley crowd. Instead Stefano had stayed and tramped round with the other people, though he felt detached from them, in search of something which drunken revels, laughter and crude music could dispel only for one day of forgetfulness. The low window opening on to the blue expanse of the sea had seemed to him the narrow, age-old window of the prison of this life. There were old men and women up there within those faded, lime-washed walls who had never left the silent piazza and the narrow streets. For them the illusion that a whole horizon could be hidden by a hand was a real one.

From behind the fan of his cards, Stefano studied the faces of the youths who had begun to converse. One of them had been born up there. All their families came from there. Those shining, intent eyes, the dark leanness of another seemed to reflect all the yearnings they had felt in that beasts' den and in that lonely prison standing isolated in the sky. The look they gave, their ingratiating smile was like a window thrown open.

"I liked it up there", said Stefano, playing a card. "It reminds me of the castles which dominate our villages".

"Would you live there, engineer?" said the dark youth, smiling.

"One lives anywhere one can, even in prison". observed Fenoaltea.

"I'd get on well with goats up there", said Stefano.

The thought that was gnawing at his heart was that the girl for him was Concia, lover of a foul old man and the flame of the village lads. But would he have her any different? Concia came from a more remote and solitary place than even the upper village. The previous day, as he contemplated a balcony with its pots of geraniums, he had dedicated them to her, ecstatically breathing in the clear, strong air which her light, tripping step recalled to him. Even the low, squalid rooms, with their ancient cupboards festooned with red or green paper, the creaking wood, the floors strewn like a stable with maize tufts and olive branches, all this brought back to his mind her goatlike face, her low forehead, a sort of brutal, timeless intimacy.

"Have you seen Don Giannino Catalano?" asked Fenoaltea, picking up the cards. "Your turn to deal, engineer".

"He hasn't come because of a visitor", said Stefano.

"He has always plenty to keep him busy while there's a *festa* on", remarked Vincenzo gravely. "You ask Camobreco what *he* thinks of his visits".

"Camobreco is the old goldsmith", explained Gaetano, "who fired a revolver shot at him from his bedroom window last year. Don Giannino Catalano had been enjoying his wife while the old boy was counting his money. Then they explained the situation by maintaining that a burglar had broken in during the night".

"Do you believe the yarn?" said one of the men.

"No one believes it, but Camobreco for the sake of peace and quiet, insists that it was a thief. A word with you before you go, engineer".

Gaetano walked along with him in the direction of the beach. The sun was beating down and Stefano wanted to hurry in order to get his clothes off as quickly as possible, but his companion was clinging on to his arm, holding him back.

"Come and have a dip Fenoaltea", said Stefano. Gaetano stood still between two houses where there was some shadow.

"This sea business is becoming a habit; how shall you get on this winter?" he asked.

"One picks up so many habits. They are my sole company".

"What about women, engineer, how do you get on without them? Haven't you got that habit?"

Stefano smiled. Gaetano, leaning against the wall, put the fingers of his right hand inside his collar.

"Go along for your bathe then, engineer, but I warn you, you have been four months away from home now, haven't you. You're a man, aren't you?"

"I try not to think about it".

"That's no reply, if you don't mind my saying so. I just wanted to warn you. Don't trust Giannino Catalano. If you want a woman, let me know".

"How does he come into it?"

Gaetano's feet shuffled off on the sandy lane; he took hold of Stefano's arm; at the corner, they came in sight of the sea.

"Do you really like that servant-girl, engineer?"

"Which one?"

"You know, Concia, the one you think looks like a goat. Eh?"

Stefano stood still in the quiet air. "Fenoaltea", he began unexpectedly.

"Don't get excited, engineer", his own plump hand slid down Stefano's arm to his hand and stroked it, "I only wanted to warn you that Don Giannino Catalano is a frequent visitor in the house where she works, and he is not a man to share a woman, especially with you who do not belong here".

That day a gang of small boys was playing about in the sea; two in particular were splashing each other to get possession of the rock. Stefano watched with distaste from where he was sitting on the sand. They were screaming at each other in their dialect, naked and brown as sea-creatures; beyond the edge of foam the whole sea, emptily clamorous, looked like a glassy land-scape before which all his senses withdrew like the shadow under his knees. He shut his eyes and the little cloud of smoke from Gaetano's pipe floated before them. The tension had become so painful that Stefano rose to move off. A boy shouted something at him. Without stopping to turn round, Stefano left the beach.

Stefano was afraid Elena might look him out that afternoon. He had desired her so much that morning when he woke up in bed and now he wanted to forget about it. He wanted to be alone, left to his own devices. The faces of the others danced round him, laughing, vague, boisterous, as they had in the uproar of the previous day: watchful and hostile as only an hour before. Those knowing looks, those insinuating fingers made his flesh shrink; he felt parts of him at the mercy of these people. Elena, for example, who was so familiar with him and had arrogated the right to cast reproachful glances at him; his secret heart, which he had so foolishly laid bare at the inn; he was suffering his nightly agonies now in the full blaze of the sun. Stefano shut his eyes and set his jaw.

He went along the embankment, almost breaking into a run. He passed before Concia's house without turning his head. When he had gone some distance and had the empty sky before him, he knew the hill rose up steeply behind his back and he felt an urge to escape.

On his right hand lay the monotonous sea. He stopped, his head bowed, and the thought that he had been afraid calmed him down. He suddenly saw the humorous side of it. He realised that Gaetano had spoken out of jealousy, putting himself in Giannino's place. It was now so patently clear that he wondered why he had suffered all those agonies, seeing he had known this at the time when Gaetano had been holding forth. There was only one answer, and it brought a smile to his lips: the invisible walls, the habit of the prison-cell which cut him off from all human contact. Those were his nightly fears.

High above the snow-capped hill hung a small cloud. The first cloud of September. He was as cheered as if he had met a friend. Perhaps the weather would change, perhaps it would rain; it would be pleasant to sit in the porch, watching the cold breeze outside, feeling the country gradually sink into inanition. In solitude — or with Giannino and his good pipe. Or perhaps without even Giannino. To remain alone there as if at his cell window. Elena now and again — but without having to talk.

FOUR

Elena did not talk much. But she looked at Stefano, endeavouring to smile at him; and her seniority in years lent it all the appearance of a mother's yearning. Stefano would have liked her to come in the morning and slip into his bed as if she were his wife, then vanish again like a dream that requires neither word nor compromise. Elena's slight hesitations, her timid way of speaking, her mere presence in fact, caused him a guilty uneasiness. Odd scraps of laconic dialogue could be heard in the room.

One evening Elena had just come in and Stefano, so as to be on his own later and enjoy a smoke in the yard, told her that someone would probably be calling during

44

the next hour or so. Elena, afraid and hurt, immediately wanted to go off and Stefano called her back. There was the sound of footsteps and someone panting behind the closed doors, and a voice called out.

"The *maresciallo*", said Elena.

"I can't believe it. Let me have a look; it can't do any harm".

"No! " exclaimed Elena, terrified.

It was Giannino. "Just a moment", called Stefano.

"It doesn't matter, engineer. I'm off for a day's sport tomorrow. Are you coming?"

When Giannino had gone, Stefano turned round. Elena was standing up between the bed and the wall in the crude light, her eyes dazzled.

"Put out the light", she stammered.

"He's gone . . .".

"Put out the light! "

Stefano put it out and moved towards her.

"I am going away", said Elena. "I shall never return".

Stefano suddenly felt sick. "Why?" he stammered, "don't you care for me?" He leaned across the bed and seized her hand.

Elena jerked her finger convulsively.

"You want to get away", she murmured. "You want to get away. You're tired of me". Stefano gripped her arm and jerked her back on to the bed. They kissed.

Dressing was not a long business this time. They approached the door arm in arm and Stefano whispered in her ear, "You will come back, Elena, you will come back, won't you? We will work it like this: you must come only if I greet you when I call at your shop. . . . And come early in the mornings when no one is about.

45

We will be safe then. No one will see you. If anyone should come — but they won't — we can make out you are doing my room . . . is that understood? Come at a time when I'm still in bed and go off quickly afterwards. Do you like coming?"

Elena smiled assent. All at once Stefano heard a voice, shy but affectionate, in his ear, "Do you really only want me to stay for a few moments? Wouldn't you like to spend a whole night with me?"

"I am a savage, you know", said Stefano suddenly, "the other way suits me best. Don't come at night. I like you that way".

Shortly afterwards, alone in the shadow, as he walked to and fro, smoking, Stefano's mind moved forward to the next day; he thought of Giannino's jocular tones. He felt a heavy, satiated fatigue following the moments enjoyed with Elena, almost as if his blood had ceased to flow, and as if the whole thing, being in the dark, had been part of a dream. But it still rankled that he had entreated her, had spoken to her and had given evidence — false though it was — of sincere and tender feelings. He felt vile and smiled a wry smile. "I am a brute". But he must tell her, however candid it might seem, that their love-making always ended in this stale-ness, this satiety. "If she'd only turn off this maternal business".

He thought of Giannino's voice, which would be calling him before dawn. Was it true about Concia? If he only had had Concia in the room with him instead of Elena. But his blood failed to quicken. "It would be just the same; not even she is really wild; she would like me to fall in love with her, and then I should have to watch out for Giannino. Who would think how fierce

Giannino was under that gentle exterior. Did he not belong to these parts?" Stefano thought it best to give up the struggle, knowing that he would be seeing him next day, speaking with him and ready to accompany him anywhere he wanted.

Meantime, next day, in the course of his walk by the sea before sunrise, Stefano thought a good deal about Concia and saw her as a wild, intangible creature, ready to yield one moment and to run away the next, whereas to a man like Giannino — with his cartridge-pouch and his white teeth gleaming in the dark — she was no doubt a devoted slave, like a brigand's lover.

Giannino laughingly apologised for having disturbed him the previous evening.

"Why?" said Stefano, surprised.

"Not because of you, engineer, but I know that in these situations women make the devil of a fuss and threaten to run away. I am so sorry I disturbed you".

A warm breeze was blowing off the sea which dulled his words, giving them an ineffable mildness. Everything was hazy and warm, and as he remembered how he was usually tormented with anxiety at that hour, he smiled and said gently, "You did not disturb me".

They passed underneath Concia's window overlooking the sea. The house looked ghost-like and shuttered, waiting for daylight to rouse it, first perhaps of all the houses that gave on to the shore. Without stopping, Giannino turned sharply to the left. "Let's take the main road; we will go up by the bathing place. Coming?"

The grasses quivered on the top of the bank. Stefano now began to discern Giannino's grey shooting jacket as he had glimpsed it for a second in the doorway of the lighted room. As he climbed behind him, he divined the old calf-length boots into which his friend's trousers were tucked.

"I've put on a jacket as I did yesterday", he said after a while.

"The main thing is not to get covered with mud".

At the first glimmer of dawn, they were still making their way inland behind the sea-shore willows. Giannino's gun, slung across his shoulders, bumped to and fro as he walked along. Clouds, shot with red flames, whirled in disarray above their heads.

"A bad time for sport", remarked Giannino without turning round, "summer over and autumn not yet here. Anyhow, we will find some blackbirds or quails".

"It's all the same to me. I am merely here as a spectator".

They now found themselves between two hills where Stefano had been before. The sparse trees and shrubs were beginning to emerge from the twilight. The bare summit of a hill stood out clearly against a cloudless sky.

"It is still summer", said Stefano.

"I would rather have wind and rain. They would bring partridges". Stefano would have liked to sit down and see the dawn break among these peaceful surroundings and watch that sky, those branches, the whole hillside turn from their present pallor to a pink suffusion. The scene changed as they walked along, and it was no longer dawn rising forth from the things around but events themselves taking charge. But Stefano enjoyed fresh air only from a window or a doorstep.

"What about a smoke, Catalano?"

While Stefano was lighting up, Giannino inspected

the treetops. A solitary twittering rose from the thicket.

Stefano said, "Could you be quite sure that I had a woman with me?"

Giannino turned a tense face towards him, his finger laid to his lips. Then he smiled by way of reply. Stefano threw the match on to the damp grass and made as if to sit down.

At length Giannino fired. He discharged his gun at the sky, at the morning, at the fleeting darkness, and the silence which ensued seemed to belong to the sun; like the lofty silence of the transparent noon over the motionless countryside.

They left the glade, and Stefano now went in front, straining his ears.

"We will go up the hill", said Giannino, "there'll be some quails there".

They climbed the bare slope, yellow with stubble. Rocks abounded and the barren crest, although not particularly high, was a long pull up. Stefano noticed tall, trembling mauve-coloured stalks on the grassy banks.

"Haven't you ever been up here before?" asked Giannino. "Behold our country. It does not even produce game".

"But you've got the sea, which produces fish".

"And we have quails — nice 'birds' too, when they're undressed! That's the only game we can get enthusiastic about".

"No doubt that's why you don't go chasing after anything else?" replied Stefano, panting.

"Would you like to fire? Over there, behind the rock, there's a quail — have a go! "

Stefano, nervous, did not see where he meant, but Giannino handed him his gun and got him to aim, putting his cheek near Stefano's.

Something certainly flew off, startled by the shot. "I am no good at this", said Stefano.

Giannino took the gun from him and fired another shot. "Got it!" he said, "you had driven it out of cover".

While they were casting about in the stubble, they heard a dry, echoing shot in the distance. "Someone else is amusing himself", said Giannino. "Look; there it is; it is only wounded".

A brown rock, apparently no different from the rest, quivered on the ground. Giannino ran up, seized it, and straightening himself up, hit it against the earth as if it had been a whip. Then he picked it up and handed it to Stefano.

"How brutal you are", remarked Stefano.

"By Jove, it's warm", replied Giannino, wiping his neck with his handkerchief.

A slight breeze still stirred the blades of grass on the banks. Stefano screwed his eyes up and descried in the distance the sun on the sea.

"Let's go", said Giannino, thrusting the bird into his game-bag. They did not come across any more quails and so, sweating and footsore, they descended to the sea-front. The trees and plants were now fully awake, casting deep shadows.

"Let's have our smoke now", said Giannino, sitting down.

The slanting rays of the sun penetrated the air and were filled with smoke like shot-silk. Giannino hardly parted his lips but allowed the blue smoke to emerge thinly almost as if it were condensing in the coolness of the air; it had a saline smell.

"I suppose you know what we call a 'quail' here?" said Giannino, closing his eyes. Stefano stared at him a few seconds. "I am ready to join in that sport too", he replied casually.

Giannino smiled knowingly and dived into his game-bag. "Here, take it, engineer; you nearly shot it yourself".

"No! "

"Why not? Get your landlady to cook it — or her daughter, so that she can say she has served you up a 'quail'! "

By way of reply Stefano said, "It's yours, Catalano. Haven't *you* got anyone who can serve *you* up a quail?"

Giannino laughed silently. "Take it, engineer. After the appetite for quails that can be read in your eyes, it will do you good! You will need pepper, though, because it will taste pretty gamey".

"It looks as if it is cocking a snook at you", said Stefano, drawing back his hand.

Giannino laughed in his beard, disturbing the symmetry of the tufts of hair, "And why not, if you please? Who is going to stop you! "

Stefano felt a sudden relief. He was free of Elena's body, now that he realised he could act as he liked and that she was his to command or reject. The amusing idea of a woman being a quail made him feel hilarious. He made a mental effort to fix it, knowing only too well that the merest trifle would suffice to dispel his happiness, itself composed of trifles: the strange hour, the suspension of time, the usual morning with the sea-bathe, his calling at the inn — all these things which at this distance away seemed to hang on a mere gesture — these were the source of his joy. Giannino alone was enough; the dawn was enough; thinking of Concia was enough. But already the thought that all that was needed was to repeat the moment to be happy — thus are vices born — dispelled the miracle. "Even Concia is a 'quail' ", he repeated, happy though uneasy.

While they were making their way across the country in the full heat of the sun, Stefano realised that the cool, fresh meadow would be for ever associated in his mind with that comic idea; Giannino's wild play on the word 'quail' would be, so to speak, permanently lodged in Concia's body. He felt grateful to these people and this country for this term if for nothing else.

"By the way, Catalano . . ." but he was interrupted by the arrival of a gun-dog which came rushing towards Giannino along the path. "Oh, there! Pierino! " cried Giannino, grabbing the animal by the collar without looking at it. A voice replied in front of them.

Where the path met the main road which descended from the mountain, they came upon the *guardia di finanza*, standing there waiting, complete with his carbine and his cloak. The dog ran joyfully ahead.

Together they took the road homeward.

"Are you a sportsman too, then, engineer?" bawled the young man.

Stefano had a picture of him with no hat on, flushed with wine and truculent on the *festa* evening. Now his appearance was slightly jaundiced — a little like his faded gold braid.

"Lucky I saw you again", he said.

Pierino winked one eye and turned to Giannino. "I must see one of you alone, but when?"

Stefano thought of the raucous bellowing the young man had raised under the starry night before finally slumping into a ditch, so shamelessly that not only a group of girls led by the parish priest but even Vincenzo and others who themselves had been joining in the singing before, slipped away so as not to be implicated. Stefano himself had moved off though he was enjoying in the darkness a sudden flash-back from remote childhood as he heard the drunkards roaring down the hill and on past the villa below.

"I was just asking Catalano why he did not come to the *festa*", said Stefano. "You seem to have had a good time there".

"Catalano works under the surface of the water", remarked Pierino.

"Naturally", joked Stefano, "who drinks anything else in this place?"

"It's too warm".

"We chaps are more innocent", said Stefano, "if there's a choice, we prefer a drop of wine".

Giannino smiled amiably. "The wine here gives you rheumatism; upon my word, I had no idea I would fall asleep in such a sweat and wake up so damn cold".

"It was your own fault", said Stefano. "You ought to have taken one of the priest's girls into the ditch with you".

"Is that what you do?"

"Me? No . . . I was listening to you when you said you were in Maremma calling up the buffaloes".

Giannino laughed. Pierino tittered and called his dog back.

"Depressing place", he roared after a time, "where the only way to be happy is to make a beast of yourself . . .".

That afternoon when he was alone in his room, Stefano suddenly threw himself full-length on his bed; he was suffering from more than boredom. His futile books on the table held no meaning for him. His future as an engineer was so remote; there would be plenty of time for that. He thought of the morning and the pleasure he had had, of which there still lingered in his nostrils the smell of a woman's body that he would always be able to recall in his times of depression. If Elena did not come in the afternoon it meant victory for him; that she accepted his wish that she should cut out those exhibitions of panic, and would let him have her without a lot of palaver.

He woke up towards evening in a stilly atmosphere, roused by the coolness of the air. But he became conscious rather of the place than of himself, as if he was not properly awake and in his dream a placid life of children, women and dogs was gradually unfolding itself in the evening breeze. He felt light-headed and irresponsible, almost like the whine of a mosquito. It must be the evening sun, he thought, that was suffusing the little piazza before the sea in a golden light. They were all there in front of the inn, ready for a game of cards and an exchange of politenesses. He was reluctant to lose hold of that moment, and did not stir, allowing an even more attractive certainty to come to the surface of his mind: that he was no longer asleep and that the peace was in fact real, that prison was now so far-off that he could fall calmly back into his drowsiness again.

FIVE

When morning came Stefano could still see in his imagination Elena's eyes dusky and solemn like her voice which in the darkness and the excitement of their evenings together he had almost forgotten. In the evening, feeling worried, he had called at her mother's shop which he had previously avoided, to let Elena know that he had not forgotten her. But Elena was out, and he could hardly understand a word of what the bundled-up old woman who spoke a local dialect said to him. Stefano had left the milk-can more as a whim than to provide Elena with a pretext for bringing it to him next morning. Hitherto Stefano had asked for the milk early in the morning from the shepherd who passed that way with his flock.

Elena came after dawn, when Stefano was already munching a piece of dry bread. She paused nervously on the doorstep, jug in hand, and Stefano realised that she had been shy of finding him still in bed.

Stefano told her to come in and smiled at her, taking the jug from her hand, caressing her discreetly at the same time, as if to indicate that there would be no need to close the shutters. Even Elena smiled.

"Do you still care about me?" said Stefano.

Elena lowered her eyes, embarrassed. Then Stefano told her that he was content to stay awhile without kissing her, although she believed that kissing was what he was after, and she was to forgive him if he was rather brusque and savage but he had lived alone so long that there were times when he hated everybody.

Elena looked at him, moved and sad. "Shall I clean up your room a bit?"

Stefano took her hand with a laugh and said, "You don't need to be so distant!" and hugged and kissed her, while Elena struggled to get free as the door was open.

Then Elena asked, "Shall I boil your milk?" and Stefano said that was a wife's job.

"But I've done it so often", replied Elena, "for people who did not even thank me for it". She was a little put out.

Stefano, who was sitting against the bed, lit his cigarette, listening to her talk. It seemed odd that these sensitive remarks should be coming from someone covered by that rough brown skirt. While she was attending to the pan on the stove, she described what she had had to put up with from the husband who had deserted her, but Stefano found himself unable to connect her present voice and hesitant glances with his memory of their closer intimacy. In the rather sweet, goat-like smell that arose from the stove, Elena seemed more in her element, becoming the average good house-wife, the rather drab presence you tolerate — along with the chickens, the broom, the housemaid. And then, deluding himself that there was nothing really in common between them except that modest outburst of confidences, Stefano managed to join in the conversation and he enjoyed at the same time an unexpected inward peace of mind.

Elena began to tidy up the room, dislodging Stefano from his place by the bed. He drank his milk and began rolling up his bathing costume in a towel. By this time Elena had swept round the place as far as the chest on which he kept the suitcase containing his things. She swung the broom round, raised her head and said sharply, "You need a wardrobe for keeping your clothes in. You ought to empty them out of your case".

Stefano was too surprised to make any objections. He had kept it there so long now, ready to close it up and set off again — but for what destination? He had talked in that vein to Giannino, hinting at prison or that piece of paper that might arrive and cause him to be hand-cuffed again and taken off — heaven knew where. Now he had dismissed it from his mind.

"I want to leave it where it is".

Elena gave him a look of surly tenderness. Stefano felt he could not go off with things as they were now, he must wind up the morning with some show of affec-tion; but as he did not want nor intend to make a habit of it, he stood hesitating in the doorway.

"Go along then", said Elena, blushing, "go and have your bathe. You are standing there like a cat on hot bricks".

"You see we can be undisturbed in the mornings", stammered Stefano. "Will you always come in the mornings?"

Elena waved her hand ambiguously by way of reply, and Stefano went off.

The days were so long now that you only had to pause a moment and look round you to have the feeling of being isolated outside time altogether. Stefano had discovered that the marine sky was getting clearer and it had a smooth appearance almost as if it were rejuvenated. Putting his bare foot on the sand was like putting it on the grass. It had got like this after a series of stormy evenings, when the rain had flooded the room. The weather was calm again now but by half-way through the morning — he went down earlier to the shore these days because several of the most assiduous callers at the inn got on his nerves — he had half forgotten the lightening, the brilliant desolation of the dog-days which seemed far away. Some mornings Stefano noticed that large fishing boats, beached on the shore with their sails furled had been pushed out into the sea at night, and not infrequently he caught fishermen he had not seen before busy disentangling their nets, still dripping with sea-water.

Pierino, the *guardia di finanza,* often came down at that cool early morning hour. Seeing those muscular limbs, little more than twenty years old, Stefano thought enviously of the rich dark blood that must nourish them, and wondered whether this Tuscan bull had not also a woman in tow. He talked a great deal. His body was made for Concia. He was pursuing this train of thought one day when he remembered that Giannino had never joined them in a bathe. Gaetano had come, fair-skinned and plump, but Giannino, never. He must be shaggy and lean, Stefano said to himself, twisted and knotty as women like men. But perhaps women did not look for muscles.

Chatting with Pierino by the door, Stefano was often light-hearted. "You're sedentary, too", he said to him one morning pointedly. But Pierino had forgotten the allusion.

"We shan't have much of a holiday", he went on, nodding his chin in the direction of a white cloud in the afternoon sky. "And they tell me it's damn cold in the winter here".

"Nonsense, I've bathed here in January".

"Ah yes, but you've got different blood in your veins". said Stefano.

"And what have you got — tertian ague?"

"Not yet, but I shall one of these nights".

"Just look at that country!" said Pierino scornfully, sweeping his arm towards the shore.

Stefano smiled. "It's no better or worse than any other place when you get to know it. Now I've been here four months it seems quite tolerable. It's a holiday for us here".

Pierino fell silent, his head lowered; he was thinking of something else. Stefano stared at the foam beneath his feet and into the sea, darkened by passing clouds.

"You see what sort of a place it is", repeated Pierino, pointing at some black dots scattered in the sea in a mottle of sunlight under the last tongue of the beach. "See that! That's the women's department".

"Perhaps they are boys", muttered Stefano. "Rot, that's the women's beach", said Pierino, getting up.

"What do they think they have got on over their bosoms, those women? If no one is interested in them, they'll never be women".

"I assure you that someone is", said Stefano, standing up. "There are as many handsome young men interested as there are houses in the place. "Things *do* happen here; you ask Catalano!"

"Do you like the women here?" asked Pierino, preparing to jump down.

Stefano pulled a wry face. "They're so scarce . . .".

"They look like goats", said Pierino and plunged in the water.

While they were dressing on the beach, Stefano said with a laugh, "There's one — the most goatlike of the lot — who lives in the grey house outside the village, beyond the bridge. Do you know her?"

"Spano's house?" asked Pierino, suddenly motionless.

"The one with geraniums at the window".

"That's it. But forgive me, I don't get the comparison. She is a lady with refined manners and regular features. How do you come to know her?"

"I've seen her carrying her pitcher to the well".

Pierino burst out laughing. "That's the servant you've been seeing".

"As a matter of fact . . .".

"What do you mean, 'as a matter of fact'? We're talking about Carmela Spano, and may I add, she's engaged to Giannino Catalano".

"Concia? . . ."

By the time they had reached the inn, Stefano had sorted the whole thing out and realised why his stupid behaviour there the morning after the *festa* had called forth so many jeers and sarcastic remarks. They had been comparing his ravings about the servant girl with what they knew of the seldom seen mistress of the house, and the addition of Giannino's name had added a spice to it all.

"I've only set eyes on your Concia once", said Pierino. "She did not seem to me as crazy-looking as you make out. I would say rather that she was the gipsy type".

At this point Gaetano came out on to the doorstep. He must have overheard their conversation because there was a twinkle in his eyes. Stefano strolled in with a casual air.

As he stood there, glancing at the newspaper open on the table, the old proprietress approached him and said that the *maresciallo* of the carabinieri had called shortly before and had inquired about him.

"In what connection?"

"You don't appear to be in a hurry".

Stefano smiled but his legs trembled. A hand fell on his shoulder. "Courage, engineer, you are innocent". It was Gaetano, laughing at him.

"Well, did he call or didn't he?"

Two of the others who were making coffee in the corner, lifted their heads. One of them said, "You look out for yourself, engineer. The *maresciallo* has electric handcuffs!"

"Did he leave any message?" asked Stefano gravely. The proprietress shook her head.

The game was exasperating that morning. Stefano was on tenterhooks all the time but he did not dare stop playing. He nodded to Giannino when the latter came in, and he got the impression that his glance was unfriendly; he attributed his own anger to the fact that Giannino had kept him in the dark about his engagement but he knew that it was really his uneasiness concerning another secret, that piece of paper which the *maresciallo* had perhaps even now in his hands, and would inexorably land him back in prison. In the agony of that thought, another one, about Concia, began to torment him; if Giannino really had no eyes for her, there was no further excuse and he ought to try his luck. He hoped in a dim way that it was not true; it was rumoured that Giannino had seduced her, or at any rate had had her in his arms under a staircase during a visit he was paying to the other woman. If indeed no one else had ever desired her, his previous imaginings had all been childish and deserved the sarcasm from the rest of them.

Giannino, bending over Gaetano's cards, said something to him. Stefano put his down and shouted, "Would you like to take my place, Catalano? I'm afraid it is going to rain and I've left my doors and windows open". He walked out under their collective gaze.

He went out into the dusty wind, but the street was deserted. He seemed to be in front of the barracks in a flash, so quickly did his thoughts race in his head. An old woman with a saucepan had stopped under the barred window of a cell, as if he had just interrupted a conversation. Her feet were bare and knobbly. A cara-biniere was leaning over a balcony on the first floor and shouting something. Stefano raised his hand, and the carabiniere told him to wait.

He came down to open the door; he was curly-haired and in his shirt sleeves; still breathless, he informed him politely that the *maresciallo* was not there. Stefano turned his eyes in the direction of the great bare corridor which, at the bottom on the first staircase landing, opened on to a small window green with foliage.

"He came to find me", said Stefano.

The carabiniere said something to the old lady, who had moved over to the door where the wind was whistling and half-closed the door in her face; then he turned to Stefano.

"Don't you know . . .?" said Stefano.

At that moment a voice could be heard, then the *maresciallo's* face appeared where the staircase curved round. The carabiniere ran up, red in the face, stam-mering that he had shut the door.

"Come along, come along, engineer, splendid", the *maresciallo* said, leaning over the rail.

In the office above he held out a piece of paper to him. "You must sign this, engineer. It is the notification of the statement to the Provincial Commission. I do not understand how they have come to send you up here without notification".

Stefano signed with a shaky hand. "Is that all?"

"Yes, that's all".

They looked at each other for a while in the quiet of the office.

"Nothing else?" asked Stefano.

"Nothing else", shouted the *maresciallo*, eyeing him doubtfully, "Unless you have been here before without knowing it! But you know *this* time! "

Stefano made his way home, oblivious of the wind. From the time that face had leaned over the bannister, the hope that the dreaded sheet of paper might mean freedom had made him quiver like a quicksand. He crossed the yard, his heart still pounding. closed the door behind him and entered his room as if it were a prison cell.

Against the back-wall by the bed was a small wardrobe, painted white, and standing on top of it was his suitcase. Stefano knew that it was empty and that all his belongings had been put in the wardrobe. But without showing any surprise, he continued to walk round. closing his eyes, compressing his lips, trying to get one single thought clear in his head, ignore everything else and imprint that one single thought on his retina; it had recurred so often; his only hope was to isolate it, erect it like a tower in a desert. The thought was relentless, isolated, an impassive closing of the mind to every word, the most secret enticement.

He stopped, breathless, his foot on a chair and his chin on his fist, staring at Elena's wardrobe. This was the thought: every pleasure, every contact, every abandonment to feeling should be shut up in his heart as in a prison, kept under control as if it was a vice, then nothing would show outwardly, and nothing should depend on external events; neither things nor people would have any more hold over him.

Stefano tightened his lips with a feeling of increasing bitterness growing up within him. He would no longer entertain any further hope but would anticipate every affliction, accepting it and battening on it in his isolation. He looked upon himself as being permanently in prison. He put his cramped leg down from the seat and began to walk, smiling at himself that he had had to strike an attitude in this way to renew his determination.

Elena's wardrobe was there. His few things were lovingly laid out on sheets of newspaper. Stefano remembered the evening when he had told Giannino that he had not enough confidence to unpack his case; he was too much a mere bird of passage. He had the images of Giannino, Concia and the rest of them, the sea and the invisible walls locked in his heart; he could enjoy them in silence. But Elena was more than an image, she was a body, a living body belonging to everyday life, inescapable like his own.

Stefano would now have to thank her for the jealous tenderness of her thought. But Stefano disliked talking with Elena; that dull sadness arising out of their intimacy made her hateful to him and brought back to his mind her clumsy gestures. If on some occasion Elena had only dared one gesture, one word of genuine possessiveness, Stefano would have clasped her to him. Even the pleasure that was renewed between them in the morning, a pleasure that Elena affected to consider futile, enjoying it as a duty, sapped his nerves and chained him too much to his prison. She felt she must isolate him, cut him off from every refuge.

The wardrobe was a handsome piece. It smelt of the house, and Stefano ran his hand over it as if to discharge his debt to Elena, endeavouring to express something to her.

SIX

Already on a previous occasion, one of his early morning encounters, Stefano had said to her, "I shall be going off one of these days, you know. Be sensible and don't let your affections run away with you".

"I know", Elena had said, struggling with her emotions; then, taking a grip of herself and eyeing him narrowly, "You wouldn't mind, either". When she spoke in this gloomy way, Elena's voice took on a throaty, rustic sound, homely like her rough-spun skirt thrown down on the chair. Her lips were downy, her hair hung untidily down her back like a housewife's as she bustled round the kitchen in her bodice in the early morning.

But Stefano was not to be enticed. Even more than by her harsh voice, he was repelled by the sensual and contented smile which could be read in every part of those lips and in the eyes that lay back on the pillow.

"You don't need to look", stammered Elena one time.

"We must — if we are to know what we're about".

In the morning the shutters allowed the passage of the half-light.

"It is enough that we are fond of each other", said Elena in the silence, "and I respect you as much as if we were the same flesh and blood. You know so much more than I do — I cannot pretend that it is otherwise — but I would like to be your mother. Stay as you are, without saying anything, be nice to me. When you feel affectionate, you know what to do".

Stefano remained with his eyes closed and tried to imagine the same words falling from Concia's lips, and as he lightly touched Elena, he thought of Concia's brown arm.

This had taken place when it was still summer outside. But on the evening of the day the wardrobe affair had happened, it had begun to rain while Stefano was waiting for Giannino in the inn. Gaetano muttered through his cigarette, "Not left anything open, this time, engineer, I hope?" Then they had watched the rain from the porch, and Giannino had arrived, raindrops glistening in his beard. The whole street was growing dark and muddy with rain; rivulets were washing the pebbles, the dampness penetrated to the bone. Summer was over.

"It is cold here", said Stefano. "Will it snow this winter?"

"It will snow up in the hills", said Giannino.

"We're not in Northern Italy here", said Gaetano, "you can even open the windows at Christmas".

"But you use the brazier. By the way, what exactly is it?"

"Womenfolk use it", chorused Giannino and Gaetano. Giannino went on to describe it. "It is a kind of bucket filled with twigs, ashes and live embers, fanned by the draught and left to heat the room. Then you can sit on it and keep warm. It drives the damp away all right", he laughed.

"But a person shut up as you are doesn't need it", added Gaetano. "Do you still go bathing?"

"If this rain goes on, I'll have to chuck it".

"But we have winter sunshine as well. It's like being on the Riviera".

Giannino started speaking again, "You've only to take a bit of exercise and you don't feel the winter any more. It's a shame you are not a sportsman. A hunting expedition in the early morning warms you up for the whole day".

"It's the evening that kills me", said Stefano. "I am stuck indoors in the evenings with nothing to do. This winter I shall have to be indoors by seven. It is even too early to go to bed".

"You could", said Gaetano, "if you wanted the sort of brazier most men use. That is what winter evenings were made for". Stefano and Giannino went out in the last glow of evening, and climbed up on to the roadway. "The country seems to shrink when it rains", remarked Stefano. "One feels no more desire to come out of doors".

The walls of the houses were dirty and smelly and the stone doorsteps and rotten doors offered no defence against the raw damp. The interior light which the summer had expelled from the houses and the air, was extinguished.

"What is the sea like in winter?" asked Stefano.

"Dirty weather. Excuse me, I've got to leave the road a moment to say a word to someone — are you coming along?"

They were on the terrace, standing still in front of the

tranquil and nebulous skyline, and below them, a few yards away was the house with the geraniums.

"Is that where you are going?"

"Where do you expect I'm going?"

They descended by a series of steps cut into the earth. The windows were closed, the loggia was full of dust sheets spread over the furniture. The damp gravel crunched under their feet. The door was ajar.

"You come along too", shouted Giannino. "If you are here too, they won't detain me". Stefano could hear the thud of the waves behind the house.

"Listen, *you* go in . . .".

But Giannino by that time had gone ahead and was groping for an opening hidden in the shadow. Just then there was a humming sound, almost like a tune, coming from a room which one knew must be light and face on to the sea. The door opened and in a burst of light and wind appeared a barefoot child.

A clear female voice called out something against the roar of the wind and a window was violently slammed to. The small child, clutching the door-handle, cried out, "Carmela, Carmela! " and Giannino lifted her off the ground, putting his hand over her mouth. In front of the window, wearing her soiled, striped blouse, stood Concia.

"Hush, you people", said Giannino, advancing into the kitchen and sitting the child on the table. Then he added, "Toschina, the priest will come and eat you up. You ought to call her 'signora' and not 'Carmela' ". Concia laughed quietly, opening her mouth and brushing her hair back with her arm. Her lips were gay and soft as if her head lay back on a pillow. "Listen, Concia, tomorrow you are to say that my mother has sent word that you are to come and do her work. You will say that she has spoken to you".

The child glanced at Stefano, at the same time wriggling off the table and on to the floor with a thud. Concia also eyed him while she replied to Giannino in rapid guttural words. "I will tell her, poor thing, but she has been weeping all day". Her brown throat swelled as she said it, her lips and eyes were animated but without showing any sympathy. Her forehead was so low that it made her eyes look odd. Her high hips, when not in movement, lacked their customary liveliness and grace.

The child had gone to the door, opened it, and went outside shouting. Giannino rushed after her to catch her and disappeared, followed by a loud laugh from Concia.

In the grey marine twilight, Concia crossed the kitchen with her usual gait; she was barefoot. Stefano noticed the familiar pitcher in the corner. Concia stood something on the lighted stove, and there at once arose a strong smell of herbs and vinegar.

From a long way off in the house came the sound of voices. Concia turned round unembarrassed with her quick, jerky movement; the light was already so dim that it reduced the brown and pink flesh tones on her face to a uniform colour. Stefano continued to gaze at her.

The voices from the upper room fell silent. There was an awkward pause. Concia's lips were parted, ready to laugh.

Stefano now looked at the window, then his eyes swept along the wall. It was low and sooty and the blue flame smelt of coal-gas.

"It must be cool here in summer", he brought out at last.

Concia was silent and continued to bend over the stove as if she had not heard.

"Aren't you afraid of thieves?"

Concia swung round. "Why, are you one?" she laughed.

"Neither more nor less than Giannino", said Stefano gently.

Concia shrugged her shoulders.

"Don't you like Giannino?" went on Stefano.

"I like whoever likes me".

She walked across the kitchen with a smile of disdainful satisfaction and took a soup-plate from the side-table. She turned towards the stove and tilted the pitcher, resting the rim on her hip and a little water overflowed from the plate. She walked straight through the puddle on the floor.

The little girl sidled back into the door-opening. Behind her in the shadow stood Giannino. Concia had hardly turned round when Giannino said, "This child of yours was getting herself shut in the hen-run...": then he mumbled something and laughed. Stefano became aware of a hesitating figure behind Giannino which immediately retreated when Giannino said to him, "Are you coming, engineer?"

They went out in the still, clear air without saying a word. When they were on the terrace-road, Stefano turned to look at the house and saw that one of the windows showed a light. The lantern of a fishing-boat, lit up ready for sailing, appeared against a background of faintly-coloured sea.

Giannino stood silent by his side, and Stefano, who

was still perspiring freely, remembered the tingling of his blood which on so many previous occasions had sent him off walking into the deserted countryside in search of a means of forgetting his loneliness. Those quiet afternoons seemed to belong to another age, the innocent, childish days when he had first come up against the cautious aloofness which now surrounded him.

Casually he said to Giannino, "That child who has just run off . . .".

". . . Is Concia's daughter". Giannino hastily completed his sentence. He, too, spoke calmly, staring at the houses, his thoughts elsewhere. Stefano's face broke into a smile.

"Is there anything wrong, Catalano?"

Giannino did not reply immediately. His clear eyes betrayed no emotion, only that he was miles away.

"Rubbish! " he remarked quietly.

"Rubbish?" echoed Stefano.

They came to a stop in front of the inn underneath the faint glow from the first lamp-post in the street, now empty of children. For several evenings now it had been dark when Stefano had come back.

In the room, as Stefano was confronted by the neatly made bed, he thought of Concia's bare feet taking the dust with them wherever they went. After eating some bread, olives and figs, he lit the light and from astride his chair, watched the pale glow from the windows. A vaporous humidity filled the yard, and the iron railings by the embankment were as dark as if there was no beach behind. So many thoughts crowded in upon him that the evening seemed short. Stefano sat in the dark room staring at the door.

71

Soon he realised that his imagination was roving among the days of the summer, the silent afternoons in the sweltering room, foam blown by the wind, the rough surface of the pitcher; the times when he was alone and the buzz of a fly filled earth or sky. The memory was so vivid that Stefano could only shake it off by forcing himself to think of the things that had affected him up to that day; then he heard a creaking sound and behind the window-pane appeared Giannino's rugged face.

"Sitting in the dark?" said Giannino.

"For a change", said Stefano and was silent again.

Giannino did not want him to light the lamp, and they sat down as before. Giannino also lit a cigarette. "You're lonely", he said.

"I was thinking that of all the summer my best moments have been spent here, on my own as in prison. The hardest lot can become a pleasure provided it is of our own choosing".

"Tricks of memory", said Giannino. He leaned his cheek against the chair back, staring at Stefano all the time. "We live with other people but it is when we are alone that we think of our own affairs".

Then he gave a nervous laugh. ". . . Perhaps you are waiting for someone this evening? . . . You are not going to tell me that you elected to come here? We don't choose our lot".

"It suffices if we want it before it is imposed on us", said Stefano. "It is not our fate but the limits set on it. The worst fate is having to accept *them*. We should rather refuse them".

Giannino made some remark that Stefano did not catch. He stopped expectantly. Giannino said nothing more.

"You were saying?"

"Nothing. Now I know you're not expecting anyone".

"Quite true. Why?"

"You were talking in too disgruntled a vein".

"Was that the impression?"

"You say things that I would only say if I was my father".

Just then a white face rose, swaying behind the glass of the window pane. Stefano gripped Giannino's arm and lowered the glowing end of his cigarette out of sight. Giannino did not move.

The intent face slipped by the window like a shadow on the water. The door shut and Stefano recognised Elena's hesitant manner. He locked the door every night and she knew it. She must think he was outside.

The chilly air from outside came in through the opening. The face hesitated a while, vague and unreal; then the door closed with a squeak. Giannino shifted his arm, and Stefano whispered, "Hush!" She had gone again.

"I've ruined your evening", said Giannino in the silence.

"It is because of the wardrobe; she came to be thanked". As he turned round, he caught a glimpse of her clear silhouette. Giannino spun round too and said, "Fate has been pretty kind to you".

"You can be sure of one thing, Catalano, you haven't ruined my evening".

"Do you think so? A woman who doesn't come in when she finds the door open, is a rare treasure". He threw down his cigarette and rose to his feet. "A rare thing, engineer. And she makes your bed for you and presents you with wardrobes! You are better off than if you were married".

73

"Not unlike your situation, Catalano".

He thought Giannino was going to light the lamp but it was not so. He heard him moving about, walking up and down; then he saw him approach the door and lean against it, his profile outlined against the glass pane.

"You've been right down in the dumps today, haven't you?" he remarked in a toneless voice. "I can't think why I took you along to that house".

Stefano hesitated. "I am grateful all the same. But I think you are the one that has been fed up".

"I ought not to have taken you", repeated Giannino.

"Why, are you jealous?"

Giannino did not smile. "I *am* fed up. Having to feel ashamed of every woman. That is a fate, too".

"Forgive me, Catalano", said Stefano, appeased, "but I know nothing about women or about you. There are so many in this house that I shall be somewhat embarrassed as to how to behave. If you will insist on feeling ashamed, could you first explain to me why?"

Giannino's profile suddenly disappeared as he turned away.

"As far as I'm concerned", continued Stefano, "even little Foschina may be your daughter. I am completely in the dark".

Giannino laughed in his nervous manner. "She is not my daughter", he said between closed teeth, "but she is almost my sister-in-law, being old Spano's daughter. Did you know?"

"I do not know the old man. I know nothing about it all".

"The old man is dead", said Giannino and did not restrain a laugh. "A tough chap who was still begetting

74

children at the age of seventy. He was a friend of my father's and knew what he was about. When he died, the women took the girl and the daughter into their own home — to look after her as guardians, out of jealousy, and so people should not talk scandal. You know what women are".

"No, not me", said Stefano.

"Spano's other daughter, who is thirty years old, is to be my wife — at any rate my father is keen on the idea".

"Carmela Spano?"

"You see, you know all about it".

"So little that I thought you had designs on Concia".

Giannino stayed silent and faced towards the windows.

"She is a daughter like any other", he said at length. "But she's an ignorant hussy. The old man took her away from the charcoal burners. Old woman Spano wanted her here so as to have her in the house".

"Is she proud?"

"She's a servant girl".

"But she's well set up — apart from her muzzle".

"You are right", said Giannino thoughtfully. "She has been in cattle stables and tending sheep so long that she has got something of the animal's muzzle about her. When we were children we used to go up to the hills with the old man Spano, and she used to lift her skirt and squat on the grass like a dog. She was the first female I ever handled: she had callosities on her backside".

"Why!" exclaimed Stefano, "what were you up to?"

"Just fooling around", said Giannino.

"And has she still got these callosities?"

Giannino nodded sulkily. "Or others like them".

Stefano smiled. "I do not understand", he said after a long silence, "what you have to be ashamed of. Your fiancée has nothing in common with her".

"Yes, I think you're right", said Giannino hastily. "I could never hold my head high again if it were not so. Do you know what?" he laughed characteristically. "I never gave the servant girl as much as a thought".

"What about it?"

"Well, it irritates me to be treated as if I was engaged to her. I know women well enough to know my duty and when you can chase them and when not. A fiancée is not a lover, and in any case she is a woman and ought to understand".

"Yet you want to cut her", said Stefano.

"What are you getting at? Don't I show myself? . . . Of course I do! It wasn't for her to put her sister-in-law on to me so she could blab about me".

"Would your sister-in-law be Foschina by any chance?"

"Toschina".

After a while Stefano began to laugh. A harsh laugh between clenched teeth to hide the fact that he was biting his lips. He was thinking of Concia curled up on the pebbles, naked and brown, and of a Carmela lying on the pebbles white and haughty. He felt Giannino's eyes on him, and stammered out, "If the brat annoys you, why don't you tell your fiancée that when you were a boy, you saw Concia's backside. She would drive her out of the house".

"You don't know us", said Giannino. "The house is united in its respect for old Spano. We all watch over Concia with a jealous eye".

SEVEN

Once more a host of thoughts crowded into Stefano's mind, so many trivial matters had occurred; all the same he was unable to concentrate on them and he stared at the door instead. He could hear Giannino's footsteps faintly in the courtyard, then they died away on the path bordering the house that rose to meet the main avenue. Through the damp doorway he could hear the thud of the sea.

Giannino had left a faint bluish trail of tobacco smoke behind him, almost as if he had stuffed some of his own beard in the bowl and had smoked it. Mingling in the night coolness, this tenuous thread savoured of the summer that had gone by, ripeness, sultry evenings, sweat. The tobacco itself was brown — like Concia's neck.

Was Elena going to come? The door was open. Even this detail reminded him of his prison cell where, whoever presented himself at the door was allowed to enter and speak to him, Elena, the goatherd, the boy who bathed, even Giannino could enter like so many gaolers, like the *maresciallo* of the carabiniere, who trusted him these days and had not called for months. Stefano was dazed by so much uniformity in this strange existence of his. The quiet summer had slipped by slowly, silently like a daydream. Among so many faces, so many thoughts, so much distress, so much peace, nothing remained except curling waves like blue reflections sweeping over a ceiling. And even that arid country, those scattered fleshy shrubs, tree-trunks and rugged boulders bleached by the sea like a pink wall, had soon ceased to affect him and had become unreal like Elena's face intersected by the window-bars. The illusion and the smell of that whole summer had insinuated themselves into his bloodstream and into his room in the same way as Concia had slipped in, even though her feet had never actually crossed the threshold.

Giannino could not be counted among the gaolers; he was more of a companion because he knew when to be silent, and Stefano liked to be alone and contemplate things that were not mentioned between them. What was peculiar to Giannino's presence was that it made each occasion pass like a quiet dream. In this it resembled encounters which take place in the street and are then sealed in the memory for ever by the surrounding tranquillity. One day Stefano had met a barefooted beggar on the road which led into the country from behind the house; the beggar jerked forward in a series of hops as if the stones burnt the soles of his feet. He was half-naked and covered with sores; his flesh was a flaming colour like his beard; the little hops like those of a wounded bird were complicated by a stick which, by getting across his legs, added to his difficulties. Stefano pictured him suddenly — he had only to think of the blazing sun and that distressful scene returned to his mind; but real distress is born of concern and that emotion did not form part of his memory. The bare flesh appeared and reappeared between the shoddy rags, defenceless and revolting, like the flesh surrounding a wound; the real body of this old man were the rags and filth, the knapsack and the sores, and as he glimpsed the raw flesh under all this, he shuddered. Perhaps the mere sight of the old man and this link with him — familiarity with his deformity and his monotonous lament — would finally make him concerned and distressed. But Stefano gave rein to his imagination instead and gradually on that scorched highway he had a vision, an outlandish, vaguely horrible object, something like a stunted and intricate Indian fig-tree, human and with limbs attached instead of branches. Horrible they were, those fat branches, amassed in a fleshy way as if the aridity of that earth could produce no other foliage, and the yellow figs which topped the leaves were in truth shreds of living flesh.

Stefano had often imagined that the heart of this world must batten on such food and that everybody must harbour within them a verdant intricacy of this kind. Even Giannino. There was a manly reserve in the latter's discreet and taciturn presence that appealed to him. Giannino was the only one who could people Stefano's solitude with things unsaid. For this reason there existed between them the eloquent silence of a first encounter.

In due course he had indeed spoken to him about the beggar, and Giannino had replied, with his eyes narrowing, "I suppose you had never seen such beggars before?"

"I now see what a beggar is".

"We have so many of them", Giannino had said. "Beggars here are like roots. They only need a touch of the sun and they quit the house and live in the way you see. There's no uniform to buy".

"With us they become proper mendicant brothers".

"Where's the difference, engineer?" Giannino had said, smiling. "It's the same thing. Our monastery is prison".

Then, as he put the clear days behind him and clouds hung darkly over the sea, Stefano's thoughts had turned to the livid flesh, to the windows where the chill wind entered and to the golden tide-washed beach. A somewhat less down-and-out tramp had appeared in the village; he was begging at the inn and had asked for a cigarette. He was a desiccated, restless specimen, muffled in an army coat that was too long for him and was always caked with mud at the bottom, underneath which emerged two feet bound up in pieces of sacking. He was satisfied with a cigarette and a glass of wine; he found soup elsewhere or subsisted on figs. He laughed sarcastically with his yellow teeth between his luxuriant beard, before begging for what he wanted.

Barbariccia, too, had had his touch of the sun, and a parish priest had harboured him, but then he had taken to the road as if by instinct. Although of a simple nature and from the hills, he was not lacking in independence and was quite capable of bestowing the term 'Cavaliere' ironically on any man who deliberately refused him a smoke. Of some he only begged a match. He removed his cap before the bald Vincenzo, touching his head and bowing. He was normally of an amiable disposition and it was said that he could not bear the damp nights.

He too had appeared one stormy morning in front of Stefano's door, doffing his cap, laughing and putting his fingers to his lips in a musulman greeting. To save time and bring him under cover from the rain, Stefano had offered him a cigarette, but Barbariccia insisted that he could only accept fag-ends, and Stefano had to search about on the floor, in the corners and in the floor-sweepings for any he could find, bending down while the beggar stood outside quietly getting wet.

"Come in! " he had said brusquely.

"I won't come in, *cavaliere*. You might find something missing, though I'm not a thief". He smelt like a dog that has been in the water. The pale morning light froze the whole room in a kind of fixed squalor between the four walls and the odd pieces of furniture.

Then Stefano had gone out into the rain and mud to have a look at the sea. On his return he had found Elena. She had put down her broom and was making the bed. He had closed the wooden shutters behind him, gone up to her, hugged her and flung her down on the bed. Although Elena resisted because her muddy shoes would dirty the counterpane, he had fondled her, talked, and had been very affectionate. They had conversed together with no outbursts of anger.

"Why had you to go out and get muddy?"

Stefano, his eyes closed, murmured, "Rain cleanses".

"Did you go out shooting with your friend?" whispered Elena.

"What friend?"

"Don Giannino . . .".

"A priest?"

Elena put her hand over his mouth. "Is it he that teaches you this sort of thing?"

"I went out to be a beggar".

"The outcast . . ." Elena's voice laughed huskily.

"It was Catalano actually who told me that all men round here have run away from home. It's a local industry . . .".

"Catalano is a lunatic. Don't believe a word he says. He has pulled the wool over his mother's eyes so often. He is an ill-bred scoundrel. You have no idea what he has done . . .".

"What, in fact?" asked Stefano, approaching.

"He is a bad lot . . . don't trust him".

Stefano listened to Elena's subdued, reproachful, almost maternal tones in the darkness. Amused, he turned over in his mind the request he had made on that past occasion. "Has he committed the offence of not bothering about you, or has he bothered you too much?" Then he felt an unexpected sense of shame at having been so callously insulting. The idea that he could be so callous with Elena annoyed and surprised him, all the more because in such cases callousness was a form of power, the only form in fact able to break down a woman's defence, the submissiveness, fraught with risk, with which she allows herself to be tracked down.

And now the wardrobe had arrived. Elena had come and had secretly withdrawn. All her strength, thought Stefano, lay in this humility, the humble submission which appeals to the affection and sympathy of the strongest. Better Concia's uptilted face, shameless and unsympathetic though it was, better those brazen glances. But perhaps Concia, too, could on occasion produce those faithful-hound looks.

Stefano roused himself in the dark, disgusted that he had allowed himself once more to become a victim of his former vacillations. He even wanted Elena back. His ironical solitude was breaking down and if he too was to give way that evening filled with so many new developments and unexpected memories, how could he put up a resistance next day? Stefano realised that he would be unable to stay alone without a struggle; but staying alone meant not wanting to struggle any longer. That was a thought which kept him company at any rate, an uncertain companion which would soon have left him.

Stefano rose and lit the lamp and his eyelids flickered. When he opened his eyes, Elena was at the door and was pushing the shutters to again with her back.

Without a word about the wardrobe, Stefano asked her if she wanted to stay the whole night. Elena looked at him, half incredulous, half amazed, and Stefano went up to her without the hint of a smile.

They could hardly squeeze into the tiny bed and Stefano thought that he would not get any sleep by daybreak. With his back against her soft body, he stared at the vague, shadowy ceiling. It was the small hours, and he could feel Elena's light breathing against his shoulders. Once more he was alone.

"Darling, we can't stay two together. I'll go", she had said, and she had not moved yet.

Perhaps she had drowsed off. Stefano put out an arm to grope for a cigarette. Elena followed him in this movement and then Stefano sat up in bed, put the cigarette between his lips and stared into the darkness, wondering whether to light up or not. When he lit the match, his closed eyelids fluttered in the deep shadows; Elena did not wake up because she was not asleep.

Stefano, who was smoking, felt himself being stared at by those half-closed eyes as if it was some game.

"Catalano saw your wardrobe this evening".

Elena did not stir.

"We saw you come; we were here in the dark".

Elena gripped his arm.

"Why did you do that?"

"So as not to compromise you".

She was wide awake now. She drew the curtain, moved up and sat beside him. Stefano freed his arm.

"I thought you were asleep".

"Why did you do that?"

"I haven't done anything. I just showed him the wardrobe". Then he went on relentlessly, "The devil teaches us not to hide things up. I don't like hypocrisy. I am glad he saw you. I do not know whether he made you out, but all mysteries end in this way".

He imagined her eyes dilated with fright, and he felt for her cheek with his hand. Instead, he felt himself being hugged violently, kissed and his whole body explored. He felt kisses on his eyes, his teeth, and he lost his cigarette. There was something childish about Elena's paroxysm. The cigarette had fallen on to the floor. Stefano finally got out of bed, pulling Elena with him. Standing there, he tried to kiss her in a calmer manner, and Elena pressed her cool body against his. Then she broke away and began to get dressed.

"Don't light the lamp", she said. "I don't want you to see me like this".

While Elena breathlessly pulled on her stockings, Stefano sat silently against the bed. He felt chilly but it was useless to get dressed again.

"Why did you do that?" stammered Elena once again.

"What?"

"Oh, I know you don't want to be beholden to me", interrupted Elena, standing up, her voice muffled by her blouse. "You don't love me — not even as you might love a mother. I understand. You cannot force yourself to love anyone merely by taking thought". Her voice became clearer and steadier as she broke free. "Light your cigarette".

Stefano, naked and embarrassed, looked at her. She

was slightly flushed and dishevelled and adjusted her petticoat casually, as if she was slipping on a kitchen apron. When she was ready, she raised her dark, almost smiling eyes.

Stefano murmured, "Are you going off?"

Elena went up to him. Her eyes had a troubled expression and they were swollen; it was just like her.

Stefano said, "Run along then and have a good cry".

Elena repressed a grimace and looked at him ambiguously, "You, poor thing, can't weep".

Stefano clasped her to him but Elena resisted. "Go back to bed".

From his bed, he said, "It is like being a child again . . .". But Elena did not bend over him or tuck in the bed-covers. She merely said, "I'll come and sweep your room for you as before. Let me know if there's anything you want. I'll have the wardrobe removed . . .".

"Don't be a fool", said Stefano.

Elena gave the faintest smile, put out the light, and went off.

Elena's voice had hardened during the last few minutes; it had the hoarse tone of someone on the defensive. Stefano, naked, had not replied. He would have liked to have heard a sob from her, but what woman fully dressed would weep in front of a naked man? The moment had passed, and that body had dressed so quickly in the dark that Stefano still had a lingering desire to caress it again, to look upon it and not to lose it. He wondered whether Elena had given him those furious kisses and that hug as she stood by

85

the bed in order to be revenged and arouse in him a desire which could no longer be satisfied. If that was so, Stefano smiled as he thought it, she had not reckoned with his thirst for solitude. Then, as it was dark, he broke into a smile and clenched his fists.

In his troubled drowsiness, Stefano's thoughts travelled elsewhere, but he could not focus them properly. As he tossed and turned in his bed, he was afraid his insomnia would continue. He was in a nightmare far more real than those of classical tradition. He pressed his cheek on the pillow patiently and noticed a faint light through the windows. He muttered affectionately, "I am sorry for you, little mother", and felt very comforted and happy to be alone.

Then this thought took shape: we resist being alone until someone else begins to suffer through our absence, real solitude is an intolerable prison. "I am sorry for you, little mother". He only had to repeat the line and the night became sweet.

Then came the wild swish as the night train went by; it caught him by surprise like a hurricane. The window-lights showed for a few seconds; when silence returned, Stefano quietly savoured a pang of his familiar nostalgia; it was a kind of aura to his solitude. His blood raced along with the train, climbing up to the coast down which he had descended handcuffed so long ago.

The pale light outside the windows had now become uniform. Now that he had definitely gone after her, he could feel affectionate about her. He could also feel compassion, he thought uncertainly, until her married blood had cooled down a bit.

EIGHT

Caught between the rain and the sun, the road lost its imperturbability, and sometimes it was very pleasant in the mornings to lean against a corner stone or a low wall on the piazza and watch the carts as they went by — loaded with hay and dry vine branches — public vehicles, countrymen riding donkeys bareback, trotting pigs. Stefano sniffed the dank, rather musty odour compounded of rain, mingled with the smell of wine-shops; and behind the station lay the sea. The shadow of the station at that hour lent the piazza a certain coolness, between a shaft of sunlight which fell from the glazed 'No Entry' door and across the peaceful, shimmering railway lines. The platform was a leap into the void. Like Stefano, the Station-master, too, lived under this void, moving to and fro on this borderland of leave-takings, in the unstable equilibrium of the invisible walls. The black trains ran along by the sea as if to escape from the dog-days they had passed through towards remote and level distances.

The station-master was a huge man, getting on in life, curly-haired and vulgar; he exchanged shouts with the porters and would burst out with unexpected guffaws, always in the midst of a bunch of people. When he crossed the piazza alone, he looked as lost as an ox without its yoke-mate. It was through him that Stefano received the first news.

He was sitting in the piazza between Gaetano and two old men, one of whom was smoking a pipe. Gaetano as he was listening to them, beckoned to Stefano, who had stopped, to come up. Stefano smiled, and just then the station master's voice growled, "Catalano may well say that there are tarts here, but then all women are tarts!"

"Why, what's happened to him?" Stefano inquired of Gaetano, whose eyes were sparkling with amusement.

"Surely you know!" said the station-master, turning red in the face. "What has happened is that he's put someone in the family way and doesn't know anything about it!" Even Stefano smiled, then he looked at Gaetano for an explanation.

When Gaetano was preoccupied he had the expression which Stefano had noticed in the days before he had got to know him. He eyed Stefano amiably and said in a confidential manner:

"The *maresciallo* sent for Catalano this morning and had him arrested . . .".

"What? . . .".

"It appears that a summons has come from San Leo charging him with indecent assault".

One of the old men interrupted: "You'll see there will be a baby too".

"The *maresciallo* of the carabinieri is a friend of ours", continued Gaetano, "and he spoke to him with respect. He arrested him in the barracks, so as not to upset his mother. Then he sent for the doctor to break it to her . . .".

There was a faint breeze smelling of coolness and the sea. The earth in the piazza was of a brownish colour, overlaid with red and shining with pools from the rain. Stefano said brightly, "He will be let out at once. Do you expect them to hold him prisoner for this nonsense?"

All four of them, including the station-master, darted hostile glances in his direction. The old man who had spoken before shook his head and they both tittered.

"You don't know what prison is", said Gaetano to Stefano.

"It is a kind of huge anteroom that you pass through into the Town Hall", explained the station-master, devouring him with his eyes.

Gaetano took Stefano by the arm and walked in the direction of the inn with him.

"In short, it is a serious charge", stammered Stefano.

"You see", replied Gaetano, "they seem resolved to make a case of it. If the girl is not pregnant, it means that they are aiming to get her married while they still have time. Otherwise they would wait for Catalano to marry his fiancée first so as to obtain more out of him by producing the child".

As they approached the inn, Stefano felt a strange sense of relief, mingled with distress and contained hilarity. He saw the accustomed faces and watched them absorbed in their games, unable to bring himself to sit down, in his anxiety to hear what they had to say about Giannino. But they did not mention him, merely exchanging the usual jokes. But he was conscious of a sense of emptiness, a futile concern, and he compared these people in his mind with the other remote world from which he had one day managed to make his escape. The prison cell was filled with the silence of the world.

But perhaps Giannino, too, was laughing in his dark and filthy cell. Possibly, as a friend of the *maresciallo*'s, he was sleeping in a room provided with a balcony and was strolling round the garden. Gaetano, with his usual air of authority, was following the game; every now and then he met Stefano's gaze with a reassuring smile.

Finally, like a sick man admitting to having a fever, Stefano admitted that he knew he was in danger. He had seduced Elena and then thrown her over; it could be considered a form of violence. But he said and thought to himself for the 'n'th time that Elena was not a minor, that she had been married and had been left high and dry more than he himself had, that she had been sincere in her fears of a scandal, and that she was simple and good. She had left him of her own free will. And she was not pregnant.

His thoughts must have betrayed him, for one of the bystanders, a mechanic and a relation of Gaetano's suddenly said, "Our engineer is thinking about his native town this morning. Courage, engineer!"

"I'm doing the same thing, engineer", interpolated Gaetano. "Upon my word, it was wonderful last year in Fossano. You've never been to Fossano, engineer, have you? To think that winter and the snow have arrived there makes me almost want to weep . . .".

"You are dying with homesickness, eh?" one of the others exclaimed.

"There was a captain who released me from the regiment, and we still write to each other".

"The said captain must have cost your father a lot of graft . . .".

"Fossano is a wild country", said Stefano. "Do you ever remember having seen a city?"

At this juncture Vincenzo and Pierino arrived together. They looked grim. But Vincenzo's browless eyes and bald head were the same as ever. Pierino, impassive in his smart uniform, said, "Beppe, run me over, will you?"

"Isn't he taking the train?" asked the mechanic.

"If they start from the station", the *maresciallo* said to me, "I will have to put the bracelets on him. Listen to me, Beppe; if old man Catalano is willing to pay for his son's journey and two soldiers and himself into the bargain, I will send him in the car and no one will see them".

"When?" said the mechanic.

"When the Court specifies", interrupted Gaetano.

"Certainly within a month. As in the case of Bruno Fava".

"Wait a minute", said Vincenzo, "it doesn't depend on the court. It will be a matter of who prefers the charge".

Stefano looked at Pierino's yellow chevrons. Pierino remarked amiably, "Are you surprised, engineer? They are all his advocates here. They all have a relative in prison".

"Why, is it like that where you come from?"

"No, it is not".

Stefano looked at their faces; they were all set, some in derisive, some serious, some stupid expressions. He thought his face must look like theirs as he said more calmly, "But hasn't Catalano got to marry a wife?" His voice came back to him in a dull, almost hostile echo.

"What does it matter?" remarked Gaetano; there was a look of assent in the others' faces. "He can't dishonour his engagement".

Pierino, leaning against the bench, looked at the floor. "You keep out of this, engineer", he said, imperiously, without raising his head.

Vincenzo, who had sat down, picked up the abandoned pack of cards and began to re-shuffle them.

"Don Catalano was careless", he said suddenly. "The

girl was sixteen and told the old folk. She will appear in the court dangling a baby boy".

"If it is a boy! " said Gaetano quietly.

"The San Leo people claim it was a case of criminal assault".

"There'll be time enough before it is born. Do you think they will really keep him in prison meantime? Ciccio Carmelo was kept in custody for a year . . .".

Stefano went down to the beach which was dreary and mottled with sunlight. It was good to stay seated on a tree-stump with one's eyes half-closed, letting time drift by. Behind his warmed shoulders were chipped walls, the campanile, low rooftops, heads leaning out of windows, people walking through the streets which were as empty as the fields; then the dizzy peak of the brown-violet mountain under the sky, and the clouds. Stefano had lost his sense of fear and watched the sea, now almost hidden under the shelving shore; he smiled to himself as he thought of his first excitement. He saw clearly how he had gone wrong. Only Giannino, who would be thinking of something very different at the present time, knew about Elena. He realised that the sudden relief he enjoyed that morning arose from the quiet tedium that this fresh adventure now interrupted and from the presentiment that with Giannino vanished the ultimate obstacle to his real solitude.

Stefano felt sad and embittered and was so little able to conceal these feelings from himself that tears welled into his eyes. They were like drops that fall from a cloth that is being wrung out, and Stefano, abandoning himself to his distress, murmured, "I am sorry for you, little mother".

The sea, which had come within his field of vision,

now appeared clearly through his stupid, smarting tears, and it brought back the summer sensation of the salt waves breaking against his eyes. And then as he closed them he realised that the excitement was not yet over.

Stefano walked across the sands again and let out a kick at a fig-tree stump; he decided to get away from the sea, for it was the sea perhaps that affected his blood and his nerves. He thought that possibly the brine, the figs, the sap from the earth had been getting into his bloodstream during the months that had passed.

He followed the embankment road which ran along by the seafront, where Concia's house stood. He pulled up sharply, for he had gone over this road too many times in the grips of his torment to venture on it just now. He turned back and embarked on the main avenue which swept round below the perimeter of the hill and then inland. At any rate some trees grew down there.

Stefano had in fact no real distress or worry to think about. It was rather an uneasiness, a feeling of anxiety, as he trod the stony road, about his own impatience at a time when his condition was human and tranquil, whereas Giannino was actually suffering, yet in all probability without being consumed with this same restlessness.

As he contemplated the shadows of the clouds over the fields, Stefano understood for the first time that Giannino was in prison. He had a very precise and definite memory of a sharp order and a banging of doors and of one door in particular being slammed in his face, followed by a voice of someone passing along the corridor instead of him. It had been such a day of white clouds, the only ones visible in the sky beyond the iron bars, that had made him dream of their shadows on the unseen earth below. He switched his glance over to the fields and on to the bare and distant trees so as to savour his liberty.

Perhaps Giannino was thinking of those same fields, the same skyline, and would give anything in the world to be walking, like him, under the open sky. But it was only the first day and perhaps Giannino was laughing, and the cell was not a cell at all because from one moment to the next a mistake might be cleared up and they would tell him he was free to go, or perhaps Giannino would still be laughing behind those same bars in a year's time; he was the kind of fellow who might.

In a beam of sunlight a little man could be seen approaching, tottering forward, huddled in a long dark coat. He was on his way down from the old part of the village, leaning on a stick; it was Barbariccia. Stefano set his jaws and decided to pass him by without listening to him; but as they gradually got closer, he felt sorry for that limp, those filthy rags trailing along, those bony hands clutching his stick. But Barbariccia did not stop. It was Stefano who said something, feeling for his cigarettes, and Barbariccia, who had already gone by, replied amiably, "What's your pleasure?"; but Stefano, confused, nodded to him and went on.

Impelled by his innate compassion, Stefano allowed his eyes to pass over the rolling fields, where scattered paths or chimneys announced the presence of some huts behind the sea-front, or a group of trees. There was not a single peasant to be seen in the stubble-field. On other occasions when he had encountered them, dressed not unlike Barbariccia or sitting on a donkey's crupper, they were quick to touch their caps to him; or women bundled up in their clothes, dark, carrying baskets and followed by goats and their small brats; he had experienced and pictured in his imagination a hard life beset with trials and the most terrible loneliness, that of a whole family on a barren soil.

One day he had remarked in Fenoaltea's shop, "The old village seems like a prison erected up there for everyone to see".

"There would appear to be plenty of people here who need it", retorted Fenoaltea senior.

Stefano stopped to look at the grey houses up there. Would Giannino be thinking of them as well, dreaming of the open horizon? It occurred to him that he had never asked whether on that now distant Sunday of his arrival in front of the piazza the man sitting impassively astride a chair had been the same one who had watched him go by in his handcuffs, numb and half-doped after his journey. Giannino would now have done the same journey not in the direction of the invisible walls of a remote country place but to the city, to a real prison. The thought that every day someone went to prison, just as someone died every day, took him by surprise. These people realised it, the women, that white-skinned Carmela, the mother, Giannino's relations all saw it, Concia too. And the other girl who had been the victim of the assault and her old folk and all the rest of them, no doubt. Every day somebody went to prison, every day the four walls closed in on somebody and the remote and agonising life of solitude began. Stefano decided to think of Giannino in that way. Hotheads of his type, scarecrows like those old tramps went in every day to populate those narrow walls with their tormented bodies and their sleepless thoughts.

Half-smiling, Stefano wondered what it was that

was so essential in a sky, in a human face, a road that plunges among olive-trees to make whoever is imprisoned beat his wings against the bars with such longing. "After all, am I living such a very different life?" he said to himself with a grimace; but knowing full well that it was a lie, he clenched his teeth and sniffed the empty air.

That day while he was having a meal in the inn, he realised that he could not recollect when he had last seen Giannino. Perhaps it was yesterday in the street, or was it in the inn, or had it been the day before? He could not decide. He wanted to know because it was clear that Giannino would no longer be seen in his company — except in memory; fugitive and pathetic, like all memories, and like that of the remote Sunday in which another memory was also enshrined. Now he would really be alone and he almost found satisfaction in the idea. He fell back once more into the bitter mood of the beach.

The old proprietress who brought him his plate told him she had fruit — oranges — the first of the season. After his soup, Stefano took an orange — two in fact — and ate them with a hunk of bread, because the act of breaking off a piece of bread, chewing it, staring into space, took him back to his prison and the solitary humility of his cell. Perhaps Giannino was eating an orange at that precise moment. Perhaps he still belonged to this world and was at table with the *maresciallo* of the carabinieri.

During the afternoon Stefano went to the barracks to ask permission to see Giannino, hoping it would be refused. In entertaining this hope he was according Giannino the same treatment he would have wished for himself in like circumstances. Giannino had not yet been a prisoner long enough to need any comforts from outside, and in Stefano's view the pride of being solitary needed no other concessions. However, he went along because Pierino had been there too.

He did not stop in front of the barred windows because he did not know which Giannino's was. The *maresciallo* came to the door and received him.

This time he greeted him with a smile of indifference. "I put him in the 'shop' half an hour ago", he said quietly. "This wasn't the prison for him".

"Transferred already?"

"Yes, just".

Stefano lowered his eyes. Then he said, "A nasty business, isn't it?"

The *maresciallo's* eyes narrowed. "As far as you are concerned, he was a healthy companion. Well and good; now all you have to do is to keep away".

Stefano made as if to go off, and the *maresciallo* looked at him. Then he added, "I'm sorry".

"One is always sorry", said the *maresciallo*.

"There was only one person . . . and now they go and lock him up". The *maresciallo*, who had now become silent, suddenly burst out with, "No: I don't know who you can go out shooting with".

"I don't care a damn about the shooting".

"You would do best to keep away", said the *maresciallo*.

NINE

It was not very cold outside in the street but in the

morning and evening Stefano felt numb and chilled in the low room and he was obliged to put on a cloak which he had carried about under his arm since the spring. Sometimes there was a fading, ash-coloured light into which gusts of wind beat mercilessly. Sometimes there were afternoons of pale sunshine.

Stefano was holding a kind of bucket filled with charcoal and hot embers to get it heated up, so he could sit by it and drowse away the evening. It was a laborious business getting the charcoal red-hot; he had to stand outside in the cold, fanning a flame of branches, bending over the brazier for a long time in the wind and rain, waiting for the gas fumes from the fuel to clear.

By the time he returned indoors with the bucket he was red, stiff, sweating, livid; not infrequently there would be a sudden flash of blue flame and he had to open the door by way of precaution. He then felt the icy breeze of the sea blowing against his legs which had been roasting close to the brazier. Once evening came he was not allowed to go out for a walk to warm himself up. Not even Giannino, he reflected, could go out and he had not got a brazier.

One morning when the courtyard was a regular swamp, Stefano lay back, nibbling at a piece of bread and an orange, throwing the peel into the dead ashes, on to the hot embers, to counteract the mouldy smell of the damp walls, as he did in the evening. The sun did not come out, and there was a good deal of mud. Elena appeared meantime with a scarf over her head, accompanied by the boy and the pitcher. He had not seen her since the night of the wardrobe but although she had in fact removed it and put his things back in the suitcase, Elena had come back now and again during his absence to do the room. She appeared behind the window in her usual sulks and Stefano found it hard to believe he had ever had her in his bed. There she was, solid and pale.

Stefano was tired; a few paces took him as far as he wanted to go, he never ventured further than the beach or the inn. He slept little during the night; a restless frenzy drove him out into the cold air at dawn. That particular morning he had risen before dawn for a set purpose. He had gone out into the courtyard muffled up; there he had lit a short pipe like Giannino had under a silent black sky. The weather was harsh, but in the shadows a puff of wind arose, accompanying the twinkling of the innumerable stars. Stefano's thoughts went back to the morning of the shooting expedition before anything had happened, when Giannino was smoking, and Concia's house, ghostly, locked, waited, expectantly. But his real memory was a different one, more secret, it was a point round which the whole of Stefano's life silently glowed, and recapturing it would have meant a shock that would have taken his breath away. Stefano had not been able to sleep his last night in prison; and then he had had to wait for the final moments, his case already packed and his papers signed, in a corridor place with high, cracked walls covered with mildew, and large windows opening on to an empty sky where summer silence reigned and bright stars twinkled that he had taken for glow-worms. For months he had seen nothing but hot-baked walls behind prison bars. Then all at once he realised that he was seeing the night-sky, that his vision extended that far and that day would see him in a train, crossing a

99

summer landscape, and he would be free to walk towards invisible, human walls, for ever. That was his boundary, and the whole silent prison fell away into nothingness, into the night.

Now in the subdued tranquillity of the tiny courtyard, Stefano, smoking like Giannino and listening to the monotonous crash of the waves, had watched for the dawn. He had waited for the sky to grow pale and the clouds to change colour, his head cocked up like a boy's. But deep in his inmost heart he was troubled by the other memory, his desperate longing for a solitude which was just coming to an end. What had he done with that death and that regeneration? Perhaps he was now leading a different sort of life from Giannino's? Stefano pursed his lips, listening to the roar of the sea, monotonous in the dawn. He could take the pitcher, go out into the road and fill it at the cold, rocky spring. He could return and go back to bed. The clouds, the roofs, the closed windows, everything at that moment expressed quietness and peace, it was all as it had been when he had come out of prison. What then? It was better to stay there dreaming of going out than not to go out in reality.

Elena, standing motionless at the other side of the windows, was watching; she held Vincenzino by the hand.

Stefano beckoned them to enter, and then stared pointedly at the bare corner where the clothes-cupboard had been. Elena shrugged her shoulders and picked up her broom without a word.

Stefano gazed at them silently so long as the boy was present, Elena sweeping and the boy holding the dustpan. She seemed in no way embarrassed; her eyes, cast down, peered into the room but without avoiding his. She was pale rather than flushed.

She sent the boy outside to get rid of the dust, and Stefano stayed where he was. There was a tense silence during the boy's brief absence.

Stefano was thinking of saying something when the boy returned. After helping to make the bed, he left at last, carrying the pitcher.

Stefano became aware that he was waiting for Elena to say something and that she had turned her back on him and was busy rearranging a bed-cover with exaggerated attention. He had nothing to say. Stefano ought to have been a long way off at that hour.

The moment passed. Was she trying to lead him on, stooping over the bed, with her forehead hidden under her hair? He got the impression that her arms were motionless under the coverlet. Her head was poised almost as if she was expecting him to strike it.

Stefano took a deep breath and contained his desire. Vincenzino would be coming back at any moment. "I'm damned if I would make a bed I am not going to sleep in!" said Stefano moving away from the door against which he had been leaning.

Then, as if he had heard the boy returning, he hastily added, "It would be very nice to make love in the morning, but we must not because the evening comes and the next day and the day after that . . .".

Elena had turned round defiantly, her clenched fists behind her, resting against the bed. She said in a whisper, "No, we do not need people like her. . . Don't torture me". She swallowed suddenly and the wrinkles round her eyes went red. Stefano smiled. "We are in this world to torture each other".

The boy hurried into the doorway, carrying the pitcher in both hands. Stefano bent down, took it from him without saying a word and carried it over to below the window. Then he fumbled in his pockets for a twenty centesimi piece.

"No", said Elena, "no! He must not take it! Why should you be troubled?"

Stefano pressed the coin into his hand and took him by the shoulders and marched him out of the door, "Run along home, Vincenzino".

He closed the door and the door-shutter; he closed all the shutters and strode across in the semi-darkness. Elena fell into his arms, moaning.

As he sat in the inn, tired and satiated, Stefano thought about his power and his loneliness. He would sleep better that night, that was worth something. From now on he would always see the dawn in and smoke like Giannino in the cold, healthy night air. His power must be real if this poor Elena could smile at him through her tears, consoled. More than that he could not give her.

He exchanged a few words with the bald-headed Vincenzo and with Beppe, the mechanic, neither of whom mentioned Giannino as they awaited their drinks. "Have a glass with me?" Stefano said.

The bottle was brought; a maroon-coloured wine that looked like coffee. It tasted cold and bitter. The mechanic, his beret pulled over his eyes, toasted Stefano, who drank down two glasses and then said, "How did the journey go?" The dark eyes of the young man winked at him.

"The way to prison is an easy one, engineer".

"What was that?" murmured Stefano. "Your wine

102

must be strong. I've been a fool not to drink it before".

Vincenzo gave a wry laugh. He was a good fellow at heart.

"They allowed your application then, engineer?"

"Yes, indeed. You were right that day; did I speak to you about it?"

Stefano went out before midday to cool his brow. The road and the houses were quivering a little under an agreeable but pale sunlight. It was so simple. Why had he not thought of it before? The whole cool winter was awaiting him.

He went to Giannino's house and mounted the stone steps, inspecting the foliage in the garden, still green by the wall. As he waited, his mind went back to Concia's house, which he had not seen lately — were those geraniums still in the window? — and to Toschina and to that other unknown voice which seemed to be choking back sobs of pride behind clenched hands.

It was miserably cold in the little room with red tiles. A heavy curtain concealed a door. The small window was closed.

The mother entered, hard, impassive, her arms folded across her chest. Stefano sat down on the edge of the chair. It was he who first mentioned Giannino. The woman's steady gaze looked expectant and hardly shifted.

"Did he not say anything to you? . . ."

An exclamation came from somewhere, probably the kitchen. But without turning a hair, the old woman continued in a stammering voice, "we are in desperate straits. My husband is becoming an imbecile in his old age. He is in the dark about the whole thing".

"I don't know anything from Giannino himself but I think there has been some trouble lately".

The old mother obstinately tightened her grip across her breast.

"I suppose you know that he has got to get married?"

"Doesn't he want to then?" Stefano found himself saying. "Giannino isn't a fool; he must have known what he was about".

"Giannino *thinks* he is not a fool", remarked his mother quietly. "But he is as much a fool and a child as the other. If he weren't stupid he would have waited until after the wedding so as to have the other girl too". Her eyes had narrowed and become hard and searching. "Have you ever been to San Leo? . . . It's a country of caves, and they don't even have priests there . . . And they want to marry my son! "

"I know what prison is", said Stefano. "Maybe Giannino would marry her to get out".

The old woman smiled.

"Giannino will never be forced into marrying anyone", she murmured. "You know about prison but you don't know my son. He will leave prison still a bachelor".

"And what about the Spano woman?" said Stefano. "What has she to say?"

"Carmela Spano is the girl that will get him. She knows him. I tell you because you don't belong here. We know them both, too. They have the father's illegitimate daughter in the house and they can't look anyone in the eye".

The old woman fell silent, clutching herself and meeting his glance. She raised her eyes when Stefano got up. "We are in God's hands", she said.

"I am not without experience. If I can be of any service . . ." said Stefano.

"Thank you. We know someone. If anything happens . . .".

As usual after being indoors, Stefano wandered off for a few moments and in no particular direction just for the sake of walking. The effect of the wine had now worn off and he could make out a pale, greenish horizon between the houses. It was the sea, remote, turbulent as ever but lacking in colour as the Indian fig of the narrow path by the shore. For months now it would not lose this unnatural pallor. It was turning into the prison-cell wall again somewhat in the way Stefano had lost his summer tan.

That afternoon he could still feel the chill in his legs from the red tiled floor; it made him think of Concia's bare feet and wonder if she was still walking about barefoot on her kitchen-floor. How long had it been now since he had come across her in a shop doorway?

It was still clear when the rain began to fall on the gravel of the roadway. Tired and stiff, Stefano returned home, divested himself of his overcoat, and sitting down in front of the windows with his feet resting on the extinguished brazier, allowed his eyes to close.

There was a vague sense of well-being in this, his usual posture, like that of a boy who, having found a cave in a wood, curls up there, defying the vagaries of the elements and the wild animal-life around. It was pleasant, the murmur of rain.

That evening Stefano provided himself with a little heat away from the rain. When he took the brazier outside, the reflection of the heat warmed his face. He heated some water and squeezed himself an orange. A bitter smell filled the air when he threw the peel into the ashes. Coming back inside from the small courtyard with his hair wet was like returning to the empty cell from a walk on a rainy day. And Stefano smiled to himself as he sat down again and lit his pipe, full of gratitude for the warmth and peace and also for the solitude, which, accompanied by the hiss of the rain outside, made him drowsy.

He thought of the protracted silences, those evenings when Giannino, sitting there with his cheek resting against the back of his chair, said nothing. Nothing had changed. Even Giannino at that hour, would be sitting on his small bed waiting in silence. But he would have no stove and his thoughts would not be conducive to sleep. Or perhaps he would be laughing. Stefano thought vaguely of his mother's words and his own. Neither she nor his fiancée knew that prison teaches you to stand alone.

Without turning his head to look, Stefano felt that the whole room had been tidied up. He could still hear the groan Elena had given. He reflected that he had treated her unkindly but all the same without malice, and now he was alone, he could think about them all in a way no one thought about him.

TEN

Someone was thinking about Stefano in point of fact, but the letters which accumulated in the table-drawer did not impinge upon the realities of his life; they dwelt pathetically on what Stefano had already forgotten about himself. His replies were brief and laconic because whoever wrote to him interpreted them in their own way despite his warnings. Even Stefano himself had quietly transformed every memory and every word, and when he occasionally received a picture-postcard showing a piazza or a landscape he had previously known, he could not credit that he had ever set eyes on the place in question.

When he had drunk a little wine those winter days, Stefano would take himself along that street where the house with the geraniums stood; no longer to escape the simple excitement belonging to summer by striding towards the horizon but to help him and collect his thoughts. The wine made him mellow and gave him the quiet courage to see himself from his solitude living in that country the way he did. The self of a few moments back was like the stranger of his previous life, nay, the stranger who had once inhabited a prison-cell. That the road he was passing along was Concia's and the house hers meant little; indeed it merely roused his impatience. It was when he was thinking of the invisible barrier which had interposed itself between himself and Concia, that he had first clearly suspected his trouble and found an energetic term to describe it.

One day Barbariccia had followed him beyond the village without letting him out of those inflamed eyes of his. Stefano was in Gaetano's company, and Barbariccia stopped when they stopped and leered at them when they noticed him, always keeping at a distance. Gaetano had told him to clear off.

Stefano recalled the evening when Barbariccia appeared at his door, hesitating, motionless; he had looked round him in the courtyard and then held out a hand that clutched an unsealed envelope. The whiteness of the paper showed up between his gnarled and blackened fingers. When he gathered that it was a message, Stefano looked at the beggar, who rolled his crazy eyes at him by way of reply.

Then he read, scrawled in pencil on a sheet of squared paper.

It is idiotic for us not to see each other when we have the right to (you had better burn this paper). If you too would like to meet me and have a frank discussion, go along the mountain-road tomorrow about ten o'clock and sit down on the low wall by the last bend. A greeting of solidarity.

Barbariccia laughed, showing his gums. The words had been gone over with a wetted pencil and the sheet itself seemed to have been in the rain.

"But who is it from?" said Stefano.

"Doesn't it say?" asked Barbariccia, stretching his neck out alongside the sheet of paper. "Your fellow-countryman up there gave the instructions".

Stefano re-read the letter to impress it on his memory. Then he took a match, lit it and held the paper between his fingers so as not to burn them. He let the charred sheet fly up in front of Barbariccia's illumined face and flutter to the ground.

"Tell him I'm ill", he said, delving into his pocket, "and that I am not my own master. And here's a piece of advice: don't bring me any more letters. Eh? Tell him I burnt that one".

Stefano had vaguely hoped the note was from Concia, but he realised that he would not have bestirred himself even for her, and for a fraction of a second he saw himself for what he was. As always when unpleasant things occurred, he laughed, and Stefano without bitterness saw that his jealous solitude was really a form of cowardice. Then he had fallen into despair.

But he did not take the road leading up the hill any more. Even on this occasion he followed the road that led by Concia's house, but without stopping.

Who was it up on the hill over there? It had been before the beggar had carried out his commission. Stefano had been joking in a rather forced way with Gaetano when the latter had suddenly seized him by his wrists, holding them together as if they were handcuffed.

"Behave yourself, engineer, or else we will be sending you into quarantine too".

Stefano had broken free, and eyed him queerly. "Your friend is mad", he said to Vincenzo, who was standing at the street corner with them. "The Catalano business has gone to his head".

"I wasn't referring to him", said Gaetano with a mischievous look, "I was saying that we'll be sending you up the mountain there".

"Didn't you know", interposed Vincenzo, "that the *maresciallo* has locked up one of your colleagues, up there in the old village?"

"What's it all about?"

"Pshaw, doesn't he know?" said Gaetano. "They transferred a 'bad lot' here to keep you company and the first thing he goes and does is to make a subversive speech to the *maresciallo*. And the *maresciallo*, who has a soft spot for you, ordered him to settle in the old village so he shan't start any trouble. Didn't he tell you?"

Stefano eyed the two of them darkly, so Vincenzo added, "The *maresciallo* appears to like you, don't

worry. If he sent you up there, it wouldn't be too good.
The streets are so narrow between the houses, you
couldn't swing a cat".

Stefano said, "When did this all happen?"

"A week ago".

"I knew nothing about it".

"He's a rum chap", said Vincenzo. "He's an
anarchist".

"He's a fool", said Gaetano. "You can't speak in
that vein to the *maresciallo*. It's a term to avoid here".

"But he is not imprisoned up there", said Stefano at
length, "he can move around".

"Are you joking, engineer? He is not allowed to
come down and they don't even understand Italian up
there . . .".

"Is he young?"

"Carmineddo says he has a beard, and the priest is
none too keen on him — he's too fond of talking to the
women. He sits on the parapet wall for hours, looking
at the view. But if he as much as stretches out a hand,
they push him over . . .".

The *maresciallo* who was cycling by in the piazza,
stopped and put his feet down from the pedals. He had
let Stefano approach and had smiled at him.

"This is nothing to do with you", he had said. "Don't
you worry your head and don't leave the village. In
winter the roads are bad".

"I understand", Stefano had murmured.

Stefano at present was passing in front of Concia's
house, and his thoughts were on the wind-swept prison
up there in that tiny space cut out in the sky which
overhung the sea in the serene emptiness of the morning. Another wall had added itself to his prison; this

time it was composed of a vague terror, a guilty anxiety. Up there, on that low parapet, sat a man, an abandoned comrade. It would not involve him in much risk to go and visit him and speak the odd word. The appeal had mentioned 'solidarity'; there emerged then, wrapped though it was in that fanatic and almost inhuman jargon, which would have been expressed in the old days in the form of a precept, milder but no less serious, an invitation to visit 'the imprisoned'. There was something that caused him to smile in those words 'frank discussion' and 'rights' — and it might be that the *maresciallo* on his bicycle that day had been smiling to himself as he recalled similar ones — but his amusement was not enough to overcome his remorse. Stefano began to feel less inclined to take any risks.

For several days he was in a panic that Barbariccia would come back to find him, and he played tricks with his imagination, thinking of the anarchist and Giannino together, both imprisoned but resolute as he himself found it impossible to be. He imagined the whole world as a prison in which everyone is shut up for the most various but all valid reasons, and he found the notion comforting. The days had shortened still more, and the rains were beginning.

Once the bathing season was over, Stefano had no more baths. He walked up and down restlessly in the abandonment of his room to warm himself up, and sometimes he shaved himself when he was in a bad mood, but for several weeks now he had not stripped properly. He knew he had lost his summer tan, and his skin was now covered with a dirty whiteness, and that day when he had taken forcible possession of Elena, he had moved away as quickly as he could and had dressed in the dark, for fear he might leave an unpleasant smell if he lingered.

Elena had not been back, as far as he knew. When he had called at the shop to pay his monthly bill, Stefano had seen her serving a customer, quite impassively and then smile with a certain detachment at the efforts of the fat mamma who was trying to explain something to him in dialect. Yet he had felt her eyes fastened on him all the time with a tenseness that had ceased to be pleasant or flattering and had become one of almost greedy possessiveness. Stefano had winked at her. Elena had lowered her head. scarlet. But she had not yet come back.

In the semi-darkness of the rains, swept away only by more violent and sullen squalls, Stefano plumbed the depths of solitude. He either remained in his room by the brazier or, under the shelter of a ridiculous umbrella, went along to the inn, half-deserted as it was in the early afternoon, and ordered a bottle of wine.

But he was not long before he discovered that time and wine-drinking do not go together. It is possible to take refuge in drinking when we are not alone, or when we have something waiting for us and the evening is a special occasion. But when we drink under the watchful eyes of the unchanging and equal hours, and our drunkenness disappears with the cold light of dawn and there are further times to be got through; when our drunkenness has nothing to accompany it or lend it a meaning, then wine-bibbing becomes merely a bad joke. Stefano thought nothing could be more awful than the wine-bottle in the prison-cell of his early days. Yet he had craved for it. And certainly Giannino must be thinking about it.

Perhaps thought Stefano, Giannino would be happy to get drunk some time. Perhaps prison was nothing else than this — the impossibility of getting drunk, of destroying time, of living an evening that was different. But Stefano knew that he was different from Giannino — he had something else, a hot, insatiable lust which could make him forget the disorder of a bed and the dirt of the bed-clothes. But to begin with, at least, the prison-cell is mortifying to the flesh, like hunger or an illness.

In the darkness of those last days of the year, Stefano enjoyed the faint beginnings of a gentle warmth in his body, of a spark kindled within him amidst the total indifference of other contacts with reality or events outside. There were, all the same, dull mornings when there was nothing more exciting to do than wake up, numb with desire. It was a depressing awakening, like that of someone in prison who had forgotten his loneliness in a dream. And within the four walls of the shuttered day nothing ever happened.

Stefano spoke to Gaetano about it without any feeling of shame. "I wonder why we are so on edge in winter?"

Gaetano listened indulgently.

"Sometimes I think it is the sun and the seashore. I have soaked up so much of it this summer and now it is having its effect ... Or perhaps it's the high seasoning of the sauces ... I am beginning to understand Giannino's and all of your carnal appetites. I feel like an Indian fig-tree. I see nothing but quails".

"In other words, a man remains a man", murmured Gaetano.

"What has Pierino to say about it?" he asked the

guardia di finanzia, who was smoking against the bench, enveloped in his cloak.

"Every place has its own particular brand of malaria", someone else remarked. "Ask the *maresciallo* for leave of absence".

"Fenoaltea, bring me some quails to shoot", moaned Stefano.

They went for a few yards along the road of the olive-trees, empty and criss-crossed with streams of rain. Stefano glanced at the summit of the hill as he walked.

"Can you go up there in the winter?"

"What do you want to see, the view?" asked Pierino.

"He means just to stretch one's legs", added Gaetano uneasily.

"If you do the rounds on duty at night, as only I have to, you don't need to stretch them".

"But you are in government service", said Stefano.

"So are you too, engineer", retorted Pierino.

As Christmas approached, the place had livened up a little. Stefano had noticed snivelling boys with no shoes on, walking up to the houses, playing trumpets and triangles and singing carols in high-pitched voices. Then they would patiently wait for someone to emerge — a woman, an old man maybe — who would put out a few sweets, dried figs, oranges or some coppers for them. On two occasions they even ventured into his courtyard — and although Stefano was irritated by the noise, he was glad they had not forgotten him and gave them money and a slab of chocolate. The boys repeated the carol — they had the laughing and deep-set eyes of Giannino, of the mechanic, of all the boys in the world — and left him feeling amazed that he should have been so much moved at so small a cost.

Fenoaltea's grocer's shop did a good trade those days, and Gaetano still helped his father and his aunts behind the counter. Peasants, poor women, barefoot servant girls, folk who had no bread to eat some days were among the customers. They left their harnessed donkeys by the door and pledged their future crops if necessary in exchange for cinnamon, cloves, flour and spices for their Christmas sweetmeats. Old Fenoaltea remarked to Stefano, "This is our season. If it were not for Christmas, we too should starve".

Concia came too. Stefano was sitting on a tea-chest gazing at the pavement and the dirty facade of the inn opposite which was faintly lit up by a luke-warm sun. Concia appeared in the doorway, brazen and as straight as a young shoot; she had not changed. She had the same silly skirt round her thighs, the same sunburnt legs; she was not barefoot this time but she jerked her feet out of her slippers at the doorway without bending down. She chatted with old Fenoaltea and Gaetano and had a joke with the old man, who leaned over the counter, laughing.

Gaetano's mother, a short, grey-haired woman, began to serve Concia, who gradually turned round and eyed Stefano at the door.

"How's your little girl?" asked Gaetano's mother, wheezily.

"She's getting a big girl", answered Concia, swaying on her hips. "Her relations dote on her".

The old woman also laughed good-naturedly. Stefano only gave Concia a perfunctory nod as she went out, still smiling. As she slid her feet into her slippers, she glanced at him.

"Liking it here still?" Gaetano muttered between

closed teeth so that all the shop should not hear. His mother shook her head. Old Fenoaltea with a fat, discreet smile turned round, "She really belongs to the hills".

"Come, what next! " said the mother.

When Christmas day came, the old proprietress of the inn, Gaetano's aunt, offered him some spiced tart which they ate in all the houses. None of the usual customers called in for a chat. Stefano ate a few pieces of tart and then made his way home, comparing his own solitude with that of the anarchist up in the old village. Barbariccia had called shortly before, doffing his cap and craving Christmas alms, cigarettes, matches, especially matches. He had given no hint of any messages.

Towards evening Gaetano came to look him out in the courtyard. He had not come there before and Stefano, alarmed, left the room to talk to him at the porch.

"What's up, Fenoaltea?..."

Gaetano had come to keep his promise. He explained in a whisper that the woman had been found and everything had been fixed up with the mechanic; they had worked it in collusion — the mechanic was going to the town, would pick her up in his car and they would keep her in the tailor's shop a couple of days.

"Is this the sort of thing one should do at Christmas!" stammered Stefano with a laugh.

Gaetano, piqued, replied that it wasn't actually for Christmas day. The woman — a handsome wench — Antonino knew her — wanted forty lire; you had to quote a figure. "Do you agree to it, engineer?"

Stefano handed him the money so as to put an end to further discussion.

"I can't ask you in. It's too dirty".

"You've got it all taped here. You've got a woman to clean for you", said Gaetano volubly.

"Yet it is the first time I've chosen a woman in the dark", said Stefano, reverting to the original topic.

"We always do it like this", remarked Gaetano, shaking Stefano effusively by the hand.

Stefano was smoking his pipe one morning at the inn when he saw Gaetano and the mechanic entering furtively. Noticing Beppe's expressionless face, he thought of Giannino who had made the last journey with him. Gaetano gravely tapped him on the shoulder. "Come along, engineer". Then he remembered.

The tailor, a little red-faced man, received them in the shop very cautiously. "She's having a meal", he said, "no one's seen you, engineer, I hope. She's eating. She spent the night with Antonino".

The wooden door at the back was sticking. Stefano said, "Let us go off, we don't want to be a nuisance", and put out his pipe.

However they went in all the same and he followed suit. The tiny room had a sloping ceiling and the woman was sitting on the rumpled bed in her camisole, showing her bare shoulders. She was eating from a soup plate with a spoon. She raised her placid eyes to meet them, balancing the plate on her lap. Her feet did not reach the ground, and it made her look like a rather plump child.

"Hungry, eh?" said the tailor in a curious rasping voice.

The woman gave a smile, at first vague and stupid and then expressing a certain contentment.

Gaetano went up to her and pinched her cheek

117

between his fingers. The woman withdrew her head pettishly, and having deposited the spoon on the floor, placed her hands on her knees, and stared expectantly at the three men with what she imagined to be a smile. Stefano said, "Don't let us interrupt your meal. We are going now".

Once outside he took a deep breath of the rarefied and chilly air. "Whenever you like, engineer", Gaetano snapped out behind him.

ELEVEN

The strange thing was that although it was still winter, there were signs of spring. Some of the boys went along barefoot with their scarves round their necks. Green shoots could be seen in the ditches that bordered the bare fields; and the almond-tree stretched its pale branches against the sky.

With the rains over, even the sea became friendly and clear again. Stefano resumed his strolls along the beach in the fresh air, pretending to himself in his extravagant way that Concia, standing barefoot, that day at the shop-door, had proclaimed the end of winter. The sea looked like a smooth green field, but the mornings and nights were still frosty. Stefano had not stopped warming himself by his brazier. The country was caked mud; Stefano imagined it already assuming spring colours, turning yellow in preparation for the summer and finally coming to the end of its cycle. How many times would he see the year round up there?

Giannino, too, could tell from the colour of the sky from his tiny window, that winter was drawing to a close. How many times would he see it? Transitory and few though these indications of spring were — a cloud or a blade of grass in the courtyard — it was certain that even an undemonstrative person like himself could not resist it. Perhaps the grace of spring brought some tender memories of a woman back to his mind — perhaps Giannino was laughing that his imprisonment was due to a similar cause — certainly if Giannino was oblivious of the seasons and colours in the world, he could appreciate the beauty of a breast, a feminine gesture and a ribald joke. It was impossible to say whether or not his Carmela was relieved to think he could not at present go questing for quails.

"Don Giannino Catalano is waiting for his case to be tried in March, he sends you his best wishes and greetings, engineer", the mechanic had said.

After the departure of the little woman — on whom Stefano had not even laid a finger, merely shutting himself up in the room with her for a few minutes so as not to offend Gaetano — something occurred to Stefano which his imagination interpreted in a childish way as a mysterious compensation on the part of Providence. One evening on his return he had found a bouquet of red flowers — he did not know what they were — in a glass on his table, next to a plate containing some cold meat covered with another. The room had been done out and swept. His suitcase on the bare table was filled to the top with clean linen. In the few minutes he had spent in the woman's wretched room, Stefano, sitting on the mattress, had asked her whether she was tired. Then he had offered her a cigarette and realising that any kind of intimacy with her would be distasteful to him, he had abstained. He had just said, "I have only

119

come to say how do you do", and smiled as politely as he could. He had watched her smoke a cigarette, that plump figure with hair tumbling untidily about her shoulders and her pink brassière with its consumptive embroidery.

Stefano now saw in the peace-offering which Elena offered in this bouquet of flowers an ingenuous attempt at reconciliation, a ridiculous reward which seemed to come from fate rather than from Elena, in recognition of his good action. Naturally Annetta had respected him for his continence but Stefano had hardly had time to smile at his hypocritical ingenuousness before he was overcome by a sudden fear. The panic he had felt on the beach, his thoughts about the Indian fig-tree, the green sap that had got into his veins. The suspicion of that morning when he had first heard about Giannino and had walked about restlessly as he felt himself permeated by the spirit of this land. "At any rate I am not weeping this time".

Not only was he not weeping but his agitation had a certain gay irresponsibility about it. He had been almost frightened that a good action could be obscurely rewarded with a bunch of flowers. But now he had found the explanation of his feelings. It was just superstition, crass superstition, the superstition of country peasants who raise their caps to the heavens and emerge from the olive grove on an ass's back.

With some mortification Stefano endeavoured to assess Elena's gesture now that he knew she was at his beck and call. Meantime he ate his supper of roast meat off the plate and found it so tasty that he thought he would eat the orange and then come back to the meat.

The meat left a bitter after-taste on his tongue. He noticed it as he sucked his orange. All this seasoning business was a local tradition, especially at Christmas time. But Stefano suspected something else. For a moment he imagined Elena had wanted to be revenged and to overheat his blood. The strange red flowers seemed to point to the same conclusion. But should he ignore it in that case? Emboldened by his recent continence, he laughed at himself and began to eat with zest.

Elena caught sight of him next day as he was strolling across the yard and waited for him at the door. They exchanged an embarrassed glance. Stefano, who had had a peaceful night's sleep, stretched himself, invited her in and kissed his fingers to her. She had an almost sly expression in her eyes but at Stefano's first movement towards her, she shook her head.

"From now on I am not going to touch you any more. Does that please you?" said Stefano, and as he left he saw Elena standing there motionless and astonished in the middle of the room.

Stefano was beginning to realise the power he had gained from poor Annetta whom he had respected more by chance than anything else. Yet this power did not emanate directly from her but from his own body; it had found a new equilibrium, giving him back a peace of mind that was not merely passive. He said to himself how stupid it was that in his pride he should have tried to isolate his thoughts and leave his body to languish on Elena's breast. To be really alone it needed so little; abstinence was enough.

Gaetano and the mechanic were discussing Annetta at the inn once again. Stefano listened to them furtively, knowing that sooner or later he would have to give in.

But when that happened, he would look for Elena. He listened remorsefully in order to put his detachment to the test.

"How our friend must be dreaming of Annetta! " remarked the mechanic.

"You're lucky, engineer", said Gaetano, "you do not even miss women".

Stefano replied, "It certainly is not fair that Giannino, who is in prison for love-making, is not even allowed to indulge himself with the person who has landed him in this jam".

"Do you expect to alter the course of justice?" said the mechanic, "What would prison be like?"

"You seem to think that prison merely consists in abstinence! "

"Why, doesn't it?"

Gaetano waited pensively for an answer.

"You are wrong", said Stefano, "prison consists in becoming a scrap of paper".

Gaetano and the mechanic did not reply. Gaetano beckoned to the old proprietress to bring him the pack of cards. Then as Barbariccia came in and pestered them, the conversation languished.

Spring cheated them; the country was desolate. Some mornings on the foreshore, feeling gloomy because he could not even have a swim now, Stefano allowed his eyes to wander over towards the little houses, a harsh pink colour, as in the far-distant July days. It would come — it must come — that morning when Stefano would have his last view of the steep hill from the train. But how many summers must pass before that? Stefano even envied the anarchist stuck over there where he could see the plains, horizons, and the sea-coast looking like a tiny toy across this stretch of open, and in the distance the blue patch of the sea; everything would have for him the beauty of an unexplored country, like a dream. Whereas he himself saw merely the squalor of the narrow streets and windows, the four hovels rising perpendicularly above the abyss, and he felt ashamed of his own vileness.

Pierino, too, the *guardia di finanza*, had told him that the *maresciallo* now had complete confidence in him, Stefano, and had even wondered whether he had not been stupid rather than guilty; and Stefano began to make his way along the road that led up the hill, under the olive trees, hoping he would be spotted from up there. He had had news of the anarchist from a woman who had come down to do some shopping at Gaetano's; apparently he was playing with children in the little piazza in front of the church, sleeping in a hayloft and spending the evenings arguing in stables. Stefano had no wish to come across him — he had now settled into a routine existence, and the other's convictions and that beard of his would upset him — but he was prepared to give him the comfort of feeling he was not abandoned.

Towards evening therefore he used to walk along the road up the hill, sit down on a tree-stump that faced on to a little valley near the roadmender's hut and smoke his pipe as Giannino would have done.

On one occasion in the summer he had hardly sat down on the said stump when he had heard the sound of tramping feet, and a group of lean men — labourers — had gone by, preceded by a priest wearing a stoll. Four youths were carrying a bier on their sunburnt shoulders, sleeves rolled up, mopping their foreheads every now and then with their disengaged arm. No one

123

spoke; they advanced at an uneven pace, raising a cloud of reddish dust. Stefano had got up from the tree-stump to pay his respects to the dead stranger, and many heads had turned to look at him. Stefano remembered saying to himself that all his life he would hear the shuffling feet of that bunch of men in the tranquil cool of that dusty evening. Now he realised he had almost forgotten it.

Sometimes, especially at first, Stefano had allowed a scene, a gesture, a landscape to impress itself on his eyes and his heart, saying: look, this is going to be my most vivid memory of the past; I am going to treasure it to my dying day as symbolising all this life; then I shall really *enjoy* it". He had done this in prison, picking out one day, one moment from the rest, saying, "I must abandon myself to it, explore this moment to the full, letting it seep into me quietly in the silence because my whole life it will be *prison* and, once I am free, I shall re-discover it in myself". And these moments, once he had selected them in this way, faded from his memory.

The anarchist must have many such memories, living as he did at a perpetual window. Unless his mind dwelt on other things and prison and confinement were not for him, like the air he breathed, the very condition of his life. As he thought of him and his own past days in prison, Stefano conjured before his eyes another race, inhuman, grown as it were to the prison cell like subterranean people. Yet this creature who played with children on the piazza was at heart simpler and more human than he was.

Stefano knew that his constant anxiety and tension arose from uncertainty, from his dependence on a scrap of paper, the suitcase that stood open on his table. How many years would he remain here? If they had said for life, perhaps he could have faced his future with greater calm.

One January morning under a watery sun, a fast car sped along the road; it was loaded with suitcases. It did not slow down. Stefano hardly troubled to raise his eyes, and he revived another forgotten moment of the summer.

In the blazing midday sun a car had stopped in front of the inn. Handsome, sleek and dusty, light cream in colour, stopping with an almost human discretion, it had drawn up by the footpath out of the shadow. From it had descended a slim woman in a green jacket and wearing black horn-rimmed spectacles; a foreigner. Stefano then turned away from the beach and gazed at the deserted road from his doorway. The woman's eyes wandered all round her and finally came to rest at the door (Stefano then realised that the reflection from the sun threw it in shadow), and turning round, she had climbed back into the car, bent forward and had driven off to a faint purring sound amid a slight cloud of dust.

Sometimes Stefano felt he had been there only a few days and that all his memories were merely figments of his imagination — like Concia, Giannino and the anarchist. He listened to the chatter of bald Vincenzo at the inn while he ate, and read the newspaper up to the last moment.

"You see, engineer, 'stormy weather'. Always the same, newspapers. I ask you, isn't the sea as calm as a mill-pond today! "

Through the door-opening could be seen the pebbles on the shore and a section of Gaetano's wall, tranquil

125

under the pale sun. Some boys, hidden from view, were shouting over on the road.

"It's almost the weather for cuttle-fishing. Haven't you ever seen it? True, you arrived in June, last year . . . It's done at night with lanterns and nets. You ought to ask permission . . .".

The *maresciallo* of the carabinieri appeared in the doorway, black and red, he had his worried 'patrol-work' expression.

"I was looking for you, engineer. Have you heard the news? . . . Finish your meal, hurry up".

Stefano leapt to his feet.

"They have rejected your appeal but you have been granted a pardon. From tomorrow you are free, engineer".

During the two days while Stefano was waiting for his clearance pass, the breakdown of his habits founded on the monotonous emptiness of time, left him dazed and discontented. In a flash he had shut up the suitcase which he had been afraid he would not have time to get ready, and then had had to re-open it to change his socks. He did not dare take his leave of Giannino's mother for fear of upsetting her, seeming to flaunt his liberty. He continued to stroll between his room and the inn, incapable of undertaking a longer walk, bidding farewell in turn to each of the deserted, wistful areas of country and sea which he had so often devoured with his eyes in fits of boredom, saying, "The last time will come and with that moment I will return to life".

Gaetano and Pierino hurried to his house to see him. Stefano who had never before been so aware of the dirtiness of his room as now when he was about to leave it for the last time, let them in, and told them to sit on the bed. They laughed uproariously at the heaps of waste paper, the refuse and ashes piled in the corners of the room. Gaetano said, "Give the girls my love if you pass through Fossano". Together they discussed the times of the trains, stations and through-coaches, and Stefano asked Pierino to remember him to Giannino.

"Tell him one gets more satisfaction from leaving prison than from being shut up inside. The world on the other side of the bars is beautiful, while the prisoner's life is like life outside only somewhat more squalid".

Then he took his courage in both hands and that evening he entered the little shop at a forbidden hour. Her mother was already in bed; Elena came forward under the light of the acetylene lamp to serve him. He told her he was settling up for his room because he was leaving for home; then he paused a moment in the silence and said that no amount of money could pay for the rest.

Elena stammered out in her husky voice "One does not give affection in return for money".

I meant all the cleaning, thought Stefano to himself but he said nothing, and took her limp hand and squeezed it without lifting his eyes. Elena did not move away from the other side of the counter.

"Who is waiting for you at home?" she said quietly.

"I have no one and I shall be alone", replied Stefano, frowning slightly. "Do you want to come tonight?"

He could not sleep that night and heard the two trains go past, the night and the dawn train with a disillusioned impatience, anticipating the roar and finding it disappointing. Elena did not appear, nor did she come in the morning; the boy with the pitcher burst in instead to ask him whether he wanted him to get him some water. He must have known the news, little brat that he was, and Stefano gave him the lira that his eyes were pleading for. Vincenzino went off at the double.

In the morning he went along to the Town Hall, where they congratulated him and gave him a last letter. Then he went to the inn which was empty. He was to depart at four o'clock that afternoon.

He crossed the road to say good-bye to old Fenoaltea but he only found Gaetano, who took him by the arm and accompanied him outside, embarking on a speech, asking him to write to him if he could find a good job for him where he was going. It did not occur to Stefano to ask him what kind of work.

Then Beppe, Vincenzo, Pierino and the others arrived and they all drank together, smoked and chatted. Someone suggested a game of cards but the proposal was not adopted.

Stefano went home as soon as he had had a meal, walked across the yard, picked up his suitcase, shut it, and after a hasty glance round him, went out into the yard again. Here he tarried a moment in front of the sea which was hardly visible beyond the terrace; at this point the path made a turn and ascended to the road.

On his way back to the inn, he waved to one of the shopkeepers he knew. There was no one at Elena's door.

He found Vincenzo at the inn, and they talked about Giannino for the last time. Stefano had been considering taking a stroll by the embankment road in front of Concia's when he was joined by Pierino and the others. He waited with them.

When they had all finally entered the station, they sat down on the seat and waited patiently; at length the ringing of a bell announced the train, and Stefano fixed his gaze on the old part of the village which towered miraculously above the roof, almost within reach. Simultaneously he caught sight of the distant train, the station-master's enormous figure emerging from his office, waving them all back, and facing him, beyond the cane-field, the pale sea which seemed to expand to fill the emptiness. As the train arrived, Stefano fancied he could see all the faces and names of those who were not present whirling round in a vortex before his eyes like leaves caught up in a wind.

THE BEAUTIFUL SUMMER

ONE

Life was a perpetual holiday in those days. We had only to leave the house and step across the street and we became quite mad. Everything was so wonderful, especially at night when on our way back, dead tired, we still longed for something to happen, for a fire to break out, for a baby to be born in the house or at least for a sudden coming of dawn that would bring all the people out into the streets, and we might walk on and on as far as the meadows and beyond the hills. "You are young and healthy", they said, "Just girls without a care in the world, why should you have! " Yet there was one of them, Tina it was, who had come out of hospital lame and did not get enough to eat at home. But even she could laugh at nothing, and one afternoon, as she limped along behind the others, she had stopped and begun to cry simply because going to sleep seemed silly and robbed you of time when you might be enjoying yourself.

Whenever Ginia was taken by a fit of that kind she would unobtrusively see one or other of her girl friends home and chatter on and on until she had nothing more left to say. So when they came to say goodbye, they had really been alone for some time and Ginia would go back home quite calmed down without missing her companion too badly. Saturday evenings were of course particularly wonderful when they went dancing and next morning she could lie in. But it did not take that to satisfy her and some mornings Ginia would leave the house on her way to work just enjoying the walk. The other girls would say, "If I get back late, I find I'm sleepy next day", or "If I get back late, they give me a beating". But Ginia was never tired and her brother who was a night-worker, slept in the day-time and only saw her at supper. In the middle of the day — Severino turned over in bed when she came in — Ginia laid the table. She was always desperately hungry and chewed slowly, at the same time listening to all the household noises. As is usually the case in empty lodgings, there was no sense of urgency, and Ginia had time to wash up the dishes that waited for her in the sink, do a bit of tidying round, then lie down on the sofa under the window and let herself drowse off to the tick of the alarm-clock in the next room. Sometimes she would close the shutters so as to darken the room and feel more cut off. At three o'clock Rosa would go downstairs, pausing to scratch gently at her door so as not to disturb Severino until Ginia let her know she was awake. Then they would set off together, parting company at the tram.

The only things Ginia and Rosa had in common were that short stretch of street and the star of small pearls in their hair. But once when they were walking past a shop-window Rosa said, "We look like sisters", and Ginia saw that the star looked cheap and realised that she ought to wear a hat if she didn't want to be taken for a factory-girl; especially as Rosa who was still under her parents' thumb wouldn't be able to afford one for heaven knows how long.

On her way down to call her, Rosa came in unless it was getting too late, and Ginia let her help her tidy round, laughing silently at Severino who, like all men, had no idea what house-keeping involved. Rosa referred to him as "Your husband", to keep up the joke, but quite often Ginia's face would darken and she complained that having all the bother of a house without the husband to go with it was no fun. In point of fact she was not serious, for her pleasure lay precisely in running a house on her own just like a housewife, but she felt she must remind Rosa from time to time that they were no longer babes. Rosa, however, seemed incapable of behaving in a dignified manner even in the street; she pulled faces, laughed and turned round. Ginia could have smacked her. Yet when they went off to a dance together, Rosa was indispensable; with her easy, familiar ways and her high spirits, she made Ginia's superiority plain to the rest of the company. In that wonderful year when they began living on their own account, Ginia had soon realised that what made her different from the others was having the house to herself — Severino didn't count — and being able to live like a lady at her present age of sixteen. She let Rosa go around with her for the same reason that she wore the star in her hair, simply because it amused her. No one else in the district could be as crazy as Rosa when she wanted. She could pull everybody's leg, laughing and tossing her head back, and some evenings she did nothing but fool the whole time. And she could be as awkward as an old hen. "What's up, Rosa?" someone remarked while they were waiting for the orchestra to start up. "I'm scared" — and her eyes started out of her head — "behind there I saw an old man staring at me and waiting for me outside, I'm scared". Her partner was not convinced, "He must be your grandfather, then!" "Silly fool!" "Let's dance, come on!" "No, I tell you, I'm frightened!" Half-way round,

Ginia heard Rosa's partner shout, "You're an ignorant little fool; run away and play. Go back to the factory!" Then Rosa laughed and made everybody else laugh but as Ginia went on dancing she thought that the factory was just the sort of place for a girl like her. You had only to look at the mechanics who picked up acquaintance with them by fooling around in a similar manner.

If there was one of these around you could be quite sure that before the evening was out one of the girls would get mad or, if she was more hysterical, start weeping. They teased you just like Rosa. They were always trying to get you to go down to the meadows; it was no use talking to them, all of a sudden you had to be on the defensive. But they had their good points: some evenings they would sing and they could sing well, especially if Ferruccio came along with his guitar. He was a tall blond fellow always out of a job but his fingers were still black and rough from handling coal. It did not seem possible that those large hands could be so skilful and Ginia, who had once felt them under her armpits when they were all on their way back from the hills, carefully avoided looking at them while he was playing. Rosa told her that this Ferruccio had inquired about her on two or three occasions and Ginia had replied, "Tell him to go and clean his nails first". The next time she was hoping he would laugh at her but he had not even looked her way.

But a day came when Ginia emerged from the dressmaker's shop adjusting her hat, and found Rosa of all people in the doorway, who rushed up to her. "What on earth's the matter?" "I've run away from the factory!" They walked along the pavement together as far as the tram and Rosa did not bring the matter up

again. Ginia felt irritated and did not know what to say.
It was only when they got off the tram near the house
that Rosa mumbled that she was afraid she was pregnant. Ginia said she was a little fool and they started
arguing at the street-corner. Then it all passed off
because Rosa had only frightened herself into thinking
it. But Ginia in the meantime had got into much more
of a state than her friend, feeling she had been cheated
and left out of it as if she was a child while the rest of
them had a good time, particularly by Rosa, who did
not possess the least pride. "I'm worth two of her",
reflected Ginia, "sixteen's too soon. So much the worse
for her if she wants to chuck herself away". Although
she spoke like this, she was unable to think about it
without feeling humiliated. She could not get over the
idea that the others had gone down to the meadows
without a word to her about it while she, who lived on
her own, still felt thrilled at the touch of a man's hand.
"But why did you come and tell me about it that day?"
she asked Rosa one afternoon when they were out
together. "And who did you expect me to tell? I was
in a jam". "But why hadn't you ever told me anything
before?" Rosa, who was quite at her ease again now,
merely laughed. She changed her tactics. "It's much
nicer when you don't tell. It's bad luck to talk about it".
"She's a fool", thought Ginia, "she laughs now but only
a short while back she was going to commit suicide.
She's not grown up yet, that's what it is". Meanwhile
when she did her journeying to and fro in the street,
even on her own, she thought how they were all very
young and how you would have to be twenty years old
all of a sudden to know how to go on.

Ginia watched Rosa's lover a whole evening, Pino

with his bent nose, an undersized fellow whose only accomplishment was billiards; who never did anything and talked out of the side of his mouth. Ginia could not understand why Rosa still went to the pictures with him when she had found out what a nasty piece of work he was. She could not get that Sunday out of her head when they had all gone out in a boat together and she had noticed that Pino's back was covered with freckles as if it was rusty. Now that she knew, she recalled that Rosa had gone off with him down under the trees. She had been stupid not to see how it was. But Rosa was stupider still and she told her so once more in the cinema-entrance.

To think they had all gone in the boat so many times, had laughed and joked and the various couples lay around in each others' arms. Ginia had seen the rest of them but had failed to notice Rosa and Pino. In the hot midday sun she and Tina, the lame girl, had remained alone in the boat. The others had got out on to the bank where their shouts could be heard. Tina, who had kept on her petticoat and blouse, said to Ginia, "If no one comes along, I shall undress and sunbathe". Ginia said she would stand on guard but she found herself listening, instead, to the voices and silences from the shore. For a short time everything was quiet on the peaceful water. Tina had stretched herself full length in the sun with a towel round her waist. Then Ginia had jumped down on to the grass and walked around barefooted. She could no longer hear Amelia's voice which had retreated beyond the others. Ginia, like a fool, imagining they were playing hide-and-seek, had not looked for them and had gone back to the boat.

TWO

One knew that Amelia, at any rate, was leading a different kind of life. Her brother was a mechanic but she only put in an appearance now and again during the evenings of that summer; she did not confide in any of them but joined in with their laughter for no other reason than because she was in her twentieth year. Ginia envied her her build, for Amelia's legs showed off a good pair of stockings. She looked rather heavy round the hips in her bathing costume, however, and her features were faintly horsey. "I'm unemployed", she remarked to Ginia one evening when she was having a good look at the latter's dress, "so I have all the day before me to study my pattern. I've learnt how to cut out through working in a dressmaker's shop like you. Can you?" Ginia thought it nicer to have things specially made but did not say so. They had a stroll together that evening and Ginia accompanied her as far as her house because she felt wide-awake and sleep was out of the question. It had been raining and the asphalt and the trees had been washed clean; she felt the coolness against her cheeks.

"You like going for walks, don't you?" said Amelia, laughing. "What does your brother Severino think about it?" "Severino is working at this time. It's his job to switch on all the lights and generally attend to them". "So he's the one that floodlights all the couples, is he? What sort of a get-up does he wear — like a gas-man?" "Of course not", laughed Ginia. "He sees to all the switches at the Central Electric Works. He stands all night in front of a machine". "So you two are on your own. Doesn't he ever preach at you?" Amelia spoke with the cheerful assurance of one who knew all about men's ways and Ginia felt thoroughly at ease with her. "Have you been out of a job long?" she asked. "I have one actually. I'm being painted".

It sounded like a joke the way she said it and Ginia looked at her. "Painted, how?" "Front face, profile, dressed, undressed, I'm what's called a model".

Ginia listened with a puzzled expression so as to draw her out though she knew exactly what Amelia meant. What seemed incredible was that she should discuss it with her, for Amelia had never alluded to the matter directly in front of any of them and it was only through the concierge that Rosa had made the discovery.

"Do you really go to a painter's studio?"

"I used to", said Amelia, "But in summer it's cheaper for an artist to paint out of doors. In winter it's too cold to pose in the nude and so you hardly ever get a job then". "Do you undress then?" "Of course", said Amelia.

Then, taking Ginia by the arm, she continued, "It's lovely work; you've nothing to do except just stand listening to them talking. I used to go to an artist who had a magnificent studio and when visitors came, they all took tea. You can learn a lot posing among that set — more than at the pictures".

"Did they used to come in while you were sitting?"

"They asked permission. Women painters are best. Did you know that women painted as well? They pay a girl to pose for them in the nude. I can't think why they don't just stand in front of a mirror. I could understand it if they used a man as a model".

"But they do", said Ginia.

"I don't say they don't", said Amelia, stopping in

140

front of the door and giving a wink. "But they pay some models double. Bless you, variety's the spice of life".

Ginia asked her why she did not come and call for her sometimes, and then went homeward alone, treading on the reflections she made on the asphalt road which had nearly dried in the warm night air. "She chatters too much about her own affairs; I suppose it's being older", thought Ginia, feeling happy. "If I led her sort of life, I'd be more discreet". Ginia was a little disappointed when she realised the days were slipping by and Amelia had not called on her. It was clear enough that she had not been trying to make up to her that evening, which implies — reflected Ginia — that she tells everything to everybody and really is stupid. I expect she regards me as an infant in arms, ready to believe anything. One evening Ginia told a number of other girls that she had seen a picture in a shop for which Amelia had been the model.

They all believed it but what Ginia meant was that she had recognised her by her build, because artists intentionally disguise the face when the model is in the nude. "Do you imagine they're as considerate as that?" said Rosa, jeering at her for her simplicity. "I would be only too pleased if an artist painted me and paid me into the bargain", said Clara. Then they proceeded to discuss Amelia's looks, and Clara's brother, who had been in the boat with them, claimed that he was more handsome in the nude. They all laughed and Ginia said, "An artist wouldn't paint her if she wasn't well set up", but they ignored her remark. She felt humiliated that evening and could have wept with rage; but the days went by and the next time she met Amelia — getting off a tram — they walked along together, chatting. Ginia was more smartly dressed than Amelia, who went along carrying her hat and showed all her teeth when she laughed.

The following afternoon Amelia came to pick her up. She walked up to the open door out of the heat and Ginia spied her from the darkness inside, without being seen herself. Once the shutters were thrown open, they took their ease and Amelia, fanning herself with her hat, looked round her. "I like the idea of an open door", she remarked. "You're lucky. You can't at my place because we're on the ground floor". Then she glanced into the other room where Severino was sleeping and said, "At our place it's a regular bear-garden. Five of us — not to mention the cats — in a couple of rooms". They went out together when they were ready and Ginia said, "When you're fed up with your ground floor, come and join me, you can have some peace here". She was trying to make Amelia understand that she wasn't meaning to criticise her people in any way but was just glad that the two of them were getting on together. Amelia, however, did not say either yes or no and treated her to a coffee on the way to the tram. Ginia did not see her the next day or the day after that, but she came up one evening, hatless, sat down on the sofa and with a laugh asked for a cigarette. Ginia was finishing the washing-up and Severino was shaving He offered her a cigarette and lit it for her with his wet fingers and all three of them had a good laugh about the street-lamp business. Severino had to go off but not before telling Ginia not to stay up all night. Amelia had an amused expression on her face as she watched him go out.

"Don't you ever go to a different dance-hall?" she asked Ginia. "Our boys are all right but they hold you too tight for my liking. Like your girl-friends".

They both went down to the town-centre without hats, choosing the shady part of the streets. They had an ice to start with and as they licked it, they watched the passers-by and joked about them. Everything came easily to Amelia; she gave herself up to having a good time as if nothing else mattered and that evening the most wonderful things might happen. Ginia knew she was safe with Amelia, who was twenty and strolled along as if she owned the place. Amelia had not even put on stockings because of the heat, and when they came to a dance-saloon, the sort that has a muffled orchestra and lamp-shades on the tables, Ginia got into a panic at the thought of having to go in with her. But her fear proved groundless and she breathed again. Then Amelia said, "Don't you feel a desire to go in there?" "It's too hot and we aren't dressed for it", said Ginia, "let's go on; it's much nicer". "I quite agree", said Amelia, "but what shall we do? Don't you ever want to stand at a street-corner and laugh at the passers-by?"

"What would you like to do?"

"If we weren't women, we should have a car and by this time we would be having a bathe in the lakes".

"Let's have a walk and a chat", suggested Ginia.

"We could go to the hills and have a drink and sing, maybe. Do you like wine?"

Ginia said she didn't and Amelia looked at the entrance to the dance-saloon. "We'll have a drink, though. Come along! People who are bored have only themselves to blame". They had a drink at the first café they came to, and once they had got outside again, Ginia felt a coolness in the air she had not felt before and thought how nice it was to cool your blood with drinks in the summer heat. Meanwhile Amelia began some rigmarole about how the people who did nothing all day had at least the right to relax in the evening, but there were moments when you got frightened as you saw the time slipping by and you began to be doubtful whether it was worth while doing so much gadding about. "Don't you feel the same?"

"The only gadding about I do is going to work", said Ginia, "I can't get much fun when I haven't even time to think about it". "You're only a kid", said Amelia, "but I can't keep still even when I'm working".

"You have to when you're posing", remarked Ginia as they walked on.

Amelia began to laugh. "You've not got a clue. The cleverest models are the ones who drive the artists frantic. If you don't move every now and again, they forget you're a model and treat you as if you were a servant. Behave like a sheep and the wolf will eat you".

Ginia merely smiled by way of reply, but something was on the tip of her tongue that burnt it like brandy. Then she asked Amelia why they didn't go and sit down in the open air and have another drink. "But of course", said Amelia. They had it at the bar because it was cheaper that way.

By this time Ginia was beginning to feel warmed up and on their way out found no difficulty in saying to Amelia, "This is what I've been wanting to ask. I'd like to see you pose".

They discussed the question for a short part of the walk and Amelia laughed because, dressed or undressed, a model can only be of interest to men and hardly to another girl. The model merely stands there; what is there to see? Ginia said she wanted to see the artist paint her; she had never seen anyone handling colours and it must be nice to watch. "I don't mean today or tomorrow", she said, "I know you're out of work at present. But if you go back to some artist's studio, you must promise to take me along with you". Amelia laughed again and told her that as far as introducing her to artists, it was the least she could do; she knew where they lived and could take her there. "But they're a lousy lot, you'll have to watch out". And Ginia laughed too.

They were sitting on a bench and there were no people going by now for it was neither early nor late. They wound up the evening in a dance-saloon in the hills.

THREE

After that Amelia often called for her to go out or to have a chat. She would come into the room and talk loudly, stopping Severino from getting any sleep. When Rosa came along in the afternoon, she found both of them ready to go out. If Amelia happened to be smoking she would finish her cigarette and would give advice to Rosa, who had told her about Pino. It was obvious that she did not care to stay longer than necessary in her lodgings and having nothing else to do all day, was glad of their company. And she would tease Rosa too when they were on their own, pretending she did not believe her stories and laughing at her quite openly.

Ginia confided in Amelia when she realised that, for all her high spirits, she was really pretty wretched. Ginia could see this merely by noticing her eyes and her crudely made-up mouth. Amelia went about without stockings only because she did not possess any; the nice dress she always wore was the only one she had. Ginia felt convinced she was correct in her conclusions when she realised on one occasion that she too felt more irresponsible if she went about without a hat. The person who got on her nerves was Rosa whom she had suddenly fathomed. "Life's worth living", said Rosa, "even if you've got to go to bed when you've torn your dress". On various occasions Ginia asked Amelia why she didn't go back to posing for artists, and Amelia told her it was no good looking for a job once you were 'unemployed'.

How pleasant it would have been to have nothing to do all day long and go out for walks together in the cool of the day, but to be so smartly turned out that when they stared at shop-windows, people would stare at them. "Being free in the way I am, makes me mad", said Amelia. Ginia would have gladly paid money to hear her hold forth so eagerly on many things which she liked, because real confidence consists in knowing what the other person wants and when someone else is pleased by the same things, you no longer feel in awe of her. But Ginia was not sure that when, towards evening, they went under the porticoes, Amelia was looking at the same man as she was. Nor could she ever be really sure what hat or material she liked; there was always the possibility that she would laugh at her as she did with Rosa. Although she was alone she never said what she would like to do, or if she did talk, it was

146

never seriously. "Have you ever noticed when you're waiting for someone", she said, "all the ugly mugs and scraggy legs that go by? It's amusing". Perhaps Amelia was joking but possibly she did devote the odd quarter of an hour to doing that sort of thing, and Ginia reflected that she would be very mad to confess that evening to her great desire to see an artist painting.

When they went out nowadays, it was Amelia who chose where they should go, and Ginia obligingly allowed herself to be taken in tow. They went back to the dance-hall of the other evening, but Ginia who had enjoyed herself so much on that occasion, no longer recognised either the lighting or the orchestra; the only pleasure she got was from the fresh air that came in at the open balconies. That is to say she did not feel well enough dressed to move around among the tables down below. Amelia, however, had embarked on a conversation with a young man with whom she was evidently already on familiar terms. When the band stopped, another man dived up and waved his hand and Amelia turned round and said, "Is it you he's interested in?" Ginia was pleased to have been noticed by some-one but the youth had disappeared, and an unpleasant type who had had a dance with her before passed hurriedly by without seeing her. Ginia had the impression that the first evening they had come, they had never once sat down at a table except to get their breath back, whereas now they waited some considerable time under the window, and Amelia who was the first to take her place, said in a loud voice, "It's good fun this time too, isn't it?" Certainly no one else in the room was better dressed than Amelia and many of the women were not wearing stockings, but Ginia had a special eye for the waiters' white jackets and was impressed by the number of cars outside. Then she realised how foolish she was to hope that Amelia's artist friend might be there.

It was so hot that year that they needed to go out every evening and Ginia felt she had never known before what summer was, so pleasant was it to stroll along the avenues every night. Sometimes she thought the summer would never end and they must make haste to enjoy it together because when the season changed something was bound to happen. For this reason she no longer went to the dance hall with Rosa or to their local cinema, but sometimes she went out on her own and hurried to the cinema in the town-centre. Why should not she do it, if Amelia did? One evening Amelia called and as they were going out, remarked, "Yesterday I found a job". Ginia was not surprised. She expected it. She quietly asked her if she was beginning straight away. "I started this morning", said Amelia. "I've already done two hours". "Are you pleased?" asked Ginia.

Then she inquired what sort of picture it was going to be. "It's not a picture at all. He is just making studies. He's drawing my face. I chatter away and at intervals he dashes down a profile. It's not anything permanent". "So you're not posing then?" said Ginia. "You seem to imagine", retorted Amelia, "that posing merely consists of getting undressed and standing around". "Are you going back tomorrow?" said Ginia.

Amelia in point of fact went there the next day and for several days afterwards. The following evening she referred laughingly to it and went on to talk about the artist, how he never stood still and asked her if any other painter had ever drawn her in that way before, walking up and down all the time. "He did a nude of me this morning. He's one of those who know what they're about and arrive at their goal by gradual stages. But with four drawings they've got you taped and put away in their portfolio and have no further use for you". Ginia asked her what he was like. Amelia said, a little man. "How did you come across him?" It had been by chance. "Call for me tomorrow", said Amelia. They planned to go along together the next afternoon, Saturday.

The whole length of the street in the hot sun that afternoon, Amelia had kept her in fits of laughter. They made their way by a winding staircase into a large semi-dark room which took a little sunlight only from the back through a gap in the curtains. Ginia, her heart pounding fast, had stopped on the last stair. Amelia called out, "Good afternoon", and walked as far as the middle of the room in the half-light and a man emerged from behind the curtains, plump and with a grey goatee beard, and said, making a gesture with his hand, "Nothing doing, girls. I'm off today". He had donned a light-coloured overall which became a dirty yellow when he turned and drew the curtain back to let in a little light. "It's no use my working today, girls. I need some fresh air". Ginia had not moved from the stair. She could see Amelia's legs against the light, some distance away. Quietly she said, as if to herself, "Let's go, Amelia".

"Will this be the little friend who wants to meet me? But she's a mere babe. Let's see you in the light".

Ginia climbed the last stair, reluctantly, feeling the grey inquisitive eyes fixed on her. She could not decide whether they were the eyes of an old man or a cunning old devil. She heard Amelia's voice — brusque, irritated — saying, "But you gave us an appointment".

"What do you want to do here?" he said. "What in heaven's name? You are tired too. Work is a thing you've got to go at gently. Aren't you thankful to have a rest?"

Then Amelia went and sat down on a chair under the shadow of the curtain and Ginia found herself standing for what appeared an endless time not knowing how to respond to the glances she received from the two of them who stared at each other and then at her. The fellow gave her the impression that he was joking, but it was a private joke for himself alone. He was still talking to her; he spoke in jerks and kept repeating, "What do you want to do?" Then suddenly the diminutive figure hopped back and drew the curtains still further to one side. A smell of freshly mixed gesso and varnish filled the empty studio.

"We are boiling hot", said Amelia, "at least you can let us cool down a bit, can't he, Ginia?" As she spoke their bearded friend swung round again and opened the large skylights. Amelia who was sitting with her legs crossed, watched him and laughed. Below the window was an easel bearing a canvas covered with daubs of colour partly scraped down. "If you don't work now while it's light, when do you work?" remarked Amelia. "I bet you are going to let me down and have another model". "I let down everybody in existence", shouted the painter, lowering his chin. "Do you consider yourself any more valuable than a horse or a plant? It's work for me even when I am out walking, can't you understand that?" Meanwhile he rummaged about in

150

a chest under the easel and threw out some sheets of paper, some small boxes of colour and some brushes. Amelia jumped up from her seat, removed her hat and winked at Ginia. "Why don't you sketch my friend?" she asked laughingly. "She's never sat for anyone before". The painter turned round. "All right, I will", he said, "she's got an interesting face".

He began to walk round Ginia, keeping a short distance away, his head turned towards her. In one hand he held a pencil and with the other he stroked his beard, staring at her all the time like a cat. Ginia who was in the centre of the studio did not dare move. Then he directed her to stand in the light, and without taking his eyes off her, threw a sheet of paper on to the easel board and began to draw. A yellow cloud could be seen in the sky and some roofs of houses; Ginia fixed her eyes on the cloud. Her heart was thumping hard. She heard Amelia make some remark; she could also hear the sound of her footsteps and her rapid breathing, but she did not turn to look.

When Amelia gave her a shout to come and see the drawing, Ginia had to close her eyes to get accustomed to the semi-darkness. Then she quietly bent over the paper and recognised her hat, but her face looked like someone else's; a dreamy face, expressionless, the lips parted as if she was talking in her sleep. "A kind of abstracted look", said Barbetta, "Is it true that no one has ever drawn you before?" He got her to remove her hat and told her to sit down and chat with Amelia. As they sat there looking at each other, they felt a great desire to burst out laughing. The artist went on covering more sheets of paper. Amelia signed to Ginia, telling her to forget she was posing.

151

"Abstracted", repeated Barbetta, looking at her from the side. "One would say that the virgin profile is not yet resolved into a definite form". Ginia asked Amelia if she was not going to pose too and Amelia slowly replied, "You're his discovery today. He will certainly hang on to you".

While they were talking, Ginia asked her if they could see the drawings he had done of her on previous occasions. Then Amelia rose and looked out a portfolio at the back of the room. She opened it on her knees, saying, "Have a look!" Ginia turned over several sheets; at the fourth or fifth, she was in a cold sweat. She did not dare to say anything, feeling the grey eyes of the man behind her. Amelia, too, was looking at her expectantly, and said finally, "Do you like them?"

Ginia raised her head, forcing a smile, "I don't recognise you", she said. She proceeded to turn them over, one by one. By the time she had finished, she was more composed. After all Amelia was there in front of her, with her clothes on and smiling.

She remarked, feeling an idiot, "Did he do them?" Amelia, baffled, replied, "I certainly didn't!"

When Barbetta had finished the next batch, Ginia would have liked to have waited a little while with her eyes closed as they were dazzled by the light outside. But Amelia shouted to her to come and Ginia was astonished when she looked at the large sheet of paper in front of her. There were lots of drawings of her head, dashed down all over the sheet, some distorted, some showing an expression which she had certainly never worn, but the hair, cheeks, nostrils were true to life and definitely recognisable as hers. She turned to Barbetta,

152

who was laughing; she could not believe they were the same grey eyes of a little time back.

Then he had been letting fly at Amelia who began abusing him and insisting that an hour was an hour and that Ginia worked for a living. She repeated that she had just come along with her casually, without any intention of stealing her job. Barbetta laughed between his teeth and said he must leave them. "Come along, I'll buy you an ice. But then I'm off".

FOUR

They returned there together next morning. This time it was Amelia's turn to pose. "Look out for yourself", said Amelia, "if you take my place again. That scoundrel knows you are partial to ices and is ready to exploit that virgin business". Ginia did not feel as pleased as she had on the previous occasion and as soon as she was awake, she had thought about the sketches of herself all amongst the nudes of Amelia and how worked up she had been. She nursed the hope of getting him to give her the drawings, not so much from a wish to possess them as because she did not like the idea of them lying there among all the others for anyone to gape at. She could not convince herself that Barbetta, that plump, pompous old artist, had drawn, rubbed out, squared up Amelia's legs, back, belly and breasts. He daren't look her in the face. Those grey eyes and that lead pencil had fixed, measured and scrutinised her more shamelessly than a mirror and put an end to her gaiety and chatter.

"I hope I am not disturbing you this morning", she

said as they passed through the doorway. "Look here". said Amelia, "do you, or do you not want to see me pose? Another time I'll be careful to keep clear of respectable girls".

All the studio windows were open and the curtains drawn back and while they were waiting for Barbetta, the old servant emerged from the stairway to come and keep an eye on them. Ginia wondered whether Amelia was getting ready to sit but she could hear her arguing with the old servant and getting her to close the windows because the morning air was chilling the room. The old woman mumbled rather than spoke, her face was so scruffy and hairy that Amelia was laughing at it, quite openly.

At length Barbetta arrived, putting on his overall and rushing around. The easel was moved to the back of the studio and his palette was brought in. There was a divan-bed at the far end and they drew all the curtains except the last one so that all the light fell on to that corner. Ginia felt *de trop* in all the turmoil and she got the impression that the old woman was looking at her disapprovingly.

When the latter left the room, Amelia began undressing near the divan and Ginia began to watch Barbetta's large hand. He held a thin piece of charcoal between his fingers and he was putting in a dark background on a sheet of whitish paper pinned on the easel. Without so much as a look in her direction, Barbetta told her to sit down, and she could hear Amelia saying something. Ginia gazed through the skylight on to the roofs as if she were posing again and thought how stupid she was. She made an effort and turned round.

Her first reaction was that Amelia must be feeling

154

cold, that Barbetta hardly seemed to be looking at her and that it was she herself who was the nuisance, coming along like that out of curiosity. Amelia, a brunette, somehow looked dirty and she found difficulty in keeping her eyes on her. She was sitting on the divan with her arms against the back of a chair, her face turned away and displaying the whole of her leg and thigh and right up to her armpit. Ginia got bored after a while. She watched Barbetta rubbing out and re-drawing, saw his brow wrinkled with concentration, exchanged a smile with Amelia — but she still felt bored. But her heart began to beat again when Amelia got up for the first time to stretch herself and picked up her bathing slip which had fallen off the divan. It was the sort of foolish excitement she would have felt if they had been alone, the excitement at the discovery that they were both made in the same mould and whoever had seen Amelia naked was really seeing *her*. She began to feel terribly ill at ease.

From her head that was resting on her arm came Amelia's voice, "Hello, Ginia". It was enough to please and calm her. A moment before she had noticed a red mottling on Amelia's leg and wondered whether if she stripped, she would have markings like that. "But my skin is younger", she said. Then she asked aloud, "Has he ever painted you in colour?" It was Barbetta who replied, "Colours are not accurate. They come in the window with the sunlight. Colours do not exist indoors". "Naturally", interpolated Amelia, "you're too mean. Colours cost money!" "Excuse me!" shouted the old man, "the reason is that I have a proper respect for colour and you know nothing at all about it beyond the colour you smear on your lips. This blonde here

155

knows more about it than you". Amelia shrugged her shoulders but without shifting her head.

The sound of a siren came from somewhere beyond the roof-tops and Ginia began to stroll round. She discovered the portrait sketches of her on the window-sill but had not the courage to ask for them. As she looked through them she saw those of Amelia again and eyed them rapidly, wondering if Amelia had really assumed the poses shown, some of which almost suggested acrobatic feats. Was it possible that an old man like Barbetta could still get a kick out of sketching girls and studying their anatomy? He was badly bitten, too, she thought.

They left after twelve o'clock and were pleased to find themselves among people again and walk along properly dressed and see the lovely colours in the street which came from the sun — it was undeniable, though they did not know how — since they disappeared at night. Even Amelia's edginess had vanished and she paid for the apéritif and they dropped the subject of painters.

Ginia's thoughts turned back to them, alone on her sofa, that afternoon and others as well. Once more she saw Amelia's swarthy belly in that semi-darkness, that very ordinary face and those drooping breasts. Surely a woman offered a better subject dressed? If painters wanted to do them in the nude, they must have ulterior motives. Why did they not draw from male models? Even Amelia when disgracing herself in that way became a different person; Ginia was almost in tears.

But she mentioned nothing about it to Amelia and was merely glad that the latter was at present earning again, that she was with her once more and was quite keen to accompany her to the cinema. Amelia could now buy herself some stockings and began to take more trouble over her hair. Ginia found it a real pleasure to be going out with her again because Amelia was such a striking figure and many people turned round to have another look at her. Thus the summer drew to a close and one evening Amelia said, "Your Barbetta man is going into the country to find his colours and do some harvesting. I was beginning to find him irritating".

That evening Amelia had produced a new handbag and Ginia remarked, "Is that his parting gift?" *"Him!"* said Amelia, "don't make me laugh! It's you he would like to have back so he wouldn't need to pay".

Then they quarrelled because Amelia had kept all this back so far and now both of them were so outspoken that they parted on bad terms. "So, she's found a lover", thought Ginia as she went home alone, "she's found a lover who is giving her presents". She decided she would only make up their quarrel if Amelia came and begged her to.

Reluctantly and in defence against her boredom, Ginia tried to pick up with her former friends again. After all, by the following summer she would be seventeen and she felt she knew her way around as much as Amelia, the more so now she was out of touch with her. During the evenings, already becoming cold, she tried to put on an Amelia-act with Rosa. She often laughed openly at her and took her for long, chatty walks. She talked to her about Pino, but she had not the nerve to take her to the dance-saloon in the hills.

Amelia had certainly someone in tow; no one ever saw her. "As long as a woman has plenty of clothes", thought Ginia, "she can cut a dash. The main thing is not to let herself be seen in the nude". But she could not discuss that sort of thing either with Rosa or Clara or with their brothers, who would immediately have drawn the worst conclusion and tried to paw her about, and Ginia did not want that; she had realised now that there were better people in the world than Ferruccio or Pino. In the evenings when she was with them, they would dance and joke and chat as well, but Ginia knew that it was no different from the larking round on Sundays when they went in the boat; a light-hearted bit of fun among the lads — the effect of the sun and their singing — when it only needed one of their number to drape a towel round his waist and pretend to be a woman to set them off into fits of laughter. At present, however, the Sunday evenings were a source of irritation because Ginia on her own was unable to make up her mind and let herself be taken along with the others. She found occasional amusement in the shop when the boss required her to do the pinning on a customer's dress; some of the stories told by the more eccentric customers were so funny. It was still more amusing when her boss affected to believe them quite seriously while all the time the mirrors reflected back the malicious mockery in her face. On one occasion a young blonde arrived who gave the impression of having a car waiting for her, but if she really had, thought Ginia, she would certainly have gone to a better-class dressmaker's. She was a tall young woman but looked evasive. Ginia considered her handsome, yes, even just in her knickers and brassière she was slim and handsome. She would certainly have made a lovely picture if she had sat for an artist; perhaps she was a model, for she paraded in front of the mirrors with the same deportment as Amelia. The next day Ginia saw the invoice but as it only had her surname on it, she was no wiser. As far as she was concerned the blonde lady continued to be a model. One evening Ginia was invited in by a friend of Severino who came to the house to bring her a lamp. The next day she went to his shop. He was a young chap like Severino and she was not in awe of him because he always wore his overalls and some years before he used to take hold of her wrists and ask her if she'd like to be whirled round. Now he looked at her with his tongue between his teeth. Ginia went there because Amelia's door could be seen from his shop, but Massimo certainly had no idea why she stopped for a chat and a joke and then returned next day as well.

They were looking at the red and blue lamps and she was playing the fool. They could see people passing by through the shop-window and Ginia asked him if it was true that Amelia went about in a white dress. "How should I know?" asked Massimo. "There's such a gang of you girls. Severino will know". "Why Severino?" "Severino is fond of fillies. Is it the girl who goes about without stockings?" "Did he tell you?" asked Ginia. "What, you his sister and don't know?" replied Massimo with a laugh. "Get Amelia to tell you. Doesn't she still come to your place?"

This was all news to Ginia. The idea that Severino was sweet on Amelia, that they had talked about it and had been seeing each other ruined her day. If it was true, all Amelia's 'crush' on her had been put on. "I'm just a kid", thought Ginia, and to contain her anger, she remembered how disgusted she had been seeing her in the nude. "But is it true?" she wondered; she found it impossible to imagine Severino in love with anyone, and she was certain that if he had seen her posing that time, poor Amelia would have lost her appeal for him. "But would she in fact? But why have we to be nude?" she thought despairingly.

Towards evening she began to feel calmer and persuaded herself that Massimo had said it merely for something to say. When she was at table with Severino, she looked at his hands and broken nails, knowing that Amelia was used to something very different. Then she remained alone when the lights were out and her mind went back to the wonderful August evenings when Amelia used to come and call for her. Just then she heard her voice at the door.

FIVE

"I've come to look you out", said Amelia.

At first Ginia did not reply.

"Are you still angry with me?" asked Amelia. "Let bygones be bygones. Isn't your brother here?"

"He is out at the moment"

Amelia was wearing her old dress but her hair was well styled and had coral combs in it. She went and sat down on the sofa and suddenly asked her if she was going out. She spoke in the same tone of voice as of old but it was huskier, as if she had a cold.

"Is it me you want or Severino?" asked Ginia.

"Oh, those people. Take no notice what they say. I only want to be distracted, are you coming along?"

Then Ginia changed her stockings and they hurried

down and Amelia got her to tell her all the month's news.

"What have you been up to?" asked Ginia. "What do you think?" replied Amelia, beginning to laugh, "nothing at all. This evening I said, 'Let's go and see if Ginia is still thinking about Barbetta' ". She could not pump any more out of her, but Ginia was satisfied. "What about going to have some refreshments?" she suggested.

While they were having a drink, Amelia asked her why she had never come and dug her out. "I didn't know where to find you". "Where do you expect? At the café all day long". "You'd never told me".

Next day Ginia went to find her at the café. It was a new café under the porticoes and Ginia searched round to find her. It was Amelia finally who hailed her in a loud voice as if she were in her own house, and Ginia saw that she was wearing a smart grey coat and a hat with a veil which made her almost unrecognisable. She was sitting with her legs crossed, resting her chin on one fist as if she were posing. "Did you really want to come?" she smiled.

"Are you expecting somebody?" inquired Ginia.

"I always am", said Amelia, making room for her next to her.

"It's my job. You've got to queue up for the privilege of stripping in front of an artist".

Amelia had a newspaper on the table and a packet of cigarettes. She was evidently earning. "I like your hat but it makes you look old", said Ginia, looking her in the eyes. "I am old", said Amelia, "any objections?"

Amelia was leaning back against the mirror as if she was on a sofa. She was looking in front of her at the mirror opposite in which Ginia could also see herself, lower down. They might have been mother and daughter. "Are you always here?" she asked. "Do artists come?"

"They come when they feel inclined. There hasn't been one today".

The chandelier was illuminated and lots of people were passing by the window. Although there was plenty of cigarette smoke round about them, it was so quiet that the buzz of conversation and other sounds seemed to reach them from a long way off. Ginia noticed two girls in a corner holding court and talking to the waiter. "Are they models?" she said.

"I don't know", replied Amelia. "Will you take coffee or an apéritif?"

Ginia had always thought one should go into cafés with a male escort and she was surprised that Amelia should spend her afternoons there alone, but she found it so pleasant to get away from the shop, stroll round the arcades and have somewhere to go, that she betook herself there again the next day. If she could have been sure that Amelia liked seeing her, she would have really enjoyed it. This time Amelia caught sight of her through the café window and made a sign that she was coming outside. They took a tram together.

Amelia did not say much that evening. "They're a lot of louts", was about all she said. "Were you waiting for someone?" asked Ginia.

In the course of their parting remarks, they planned for the following day and Ginia felt convinced that Amelia liked seeing her and that if something had gone wrong, it had been for other reasons, possibly something to do with the 'uncouth louts'.

"How does it work? Does an artist come along and ask you if you are willing to sit?" she asked, laughing.

"There are some, too, who don't say anything", explained Amelia. "They don't need models".

"What do they paint then?"

"Do you know what! There's one artist who says that he applies paint as we apply lipstick! 'What do you paint when you're putting on lipstick? Well, I paint the same way', he says".

"But you paint your lips with lipstick".

"And he paints his canvas. Bye-bye, Ginia".

When Amelia talked in this mocking way with a straight face Ginia was afraid something was afoot and felt uneasy and lonely as she went home. Luckily for her, once there, she had to hurry and knock up a supper of pasta for Severino. When supper was over, it was different because night was approaching and the time for going out by herself or with Rosa. Sometimes she thought, "What sort of life am I leading? I'm always on the hop". But it was the sort of life she liked because this was the only way she could enjoy that moment's peace in the afternoon or in the evening at Amelia's café and relax. If she had not had Amelia, she would have been less tied but how could she do what she wanted now the days were no use to her and she found no more pleasure walking down the street? And it was sure to be through Amelia and not through any of the silly fools like Rosa or Clara if anything exciting did happen that winter.

She began to pick up acquaintances at the café. There was one gentleman who resembled Barbetta and when they left, he waved his hand to Amelia. He addressed them respectfully, and Amelia told Ginia that he was not a painter. A tall young man, who drew his car up in front of the arcades and was accompanied by a very smart woman, sometimes came to the bar. Amelia did not know him but said he was not a painter.

"There don't seem to be many about, do there?" she said to Ginia. "The ones who work seriously haven't time to come". So Amelia had more acquaintances among waiters than among the customers but Ginia, who was fond of hearing the latter joking together, was careful not to trust any of them too far. One who often sat with Amelia and had moved to Ginia on the first occasion without so much as a glance in her direction, was a hairy youth with a white tie and very black eyes, called Rodrigues. In fact he did not look like an Italian at all and he had a peculiar, rasping voice. Amelia talked to him as if he was a naughty boy, telling him that, if instead of squandering that lira at the café, he had kept it, he could — in ten days — have paid for a model. Ginia listened, amused, but Rodrigues now began in his hesitant voice to treat Amelia alternately as a fine lady and a spoilt child. She smiled, but sometimes she was annoyed and told him to go away. Rodrigues then moved to another table, pulled out his pencil and began to write, watching them out of the corner of his eye. "Don't pay any attention to him", said Amelia, "it's just what he'd like". So gradually Ginia got accustomed to ignoring him.

One evening they went out together with no particular aim in view. They had been for a walk; it had begun to rain and they took shelter under a doorway. They found it chilly standing still in their wet stockings. Amelia had said, "If Guido is at home, what about going along to his place?" "Who is Guido?" Amelia had then put her nose outside and craned her neck to look at the windows of the house opposite. "There's a light; let's go up, we shall be under cover". They had mounted at least to the sixth floor and had reached the attics when Amelia paused, breathless, and said, "Are you afraid?" "Why should I be?" said Ginia, "You know him, don't you?"

While they were knocking at the door, they could hear the sound of laughter inside; it was a subdued and unpleasant laugh that reminded Ginia of Rodrigues. They heard footsteps, the door opened, but they could not see anyone. "May we come in?" said Amelia.

It was Rodrigues. He was lying on a sofa against the wall under a harsh light. But there was someone else there, standing up; it was a soldier in his shirt sleeves, blond, mud-stained, who looked at them and smiled. Ginia had to lower her eyes against the glare of the lamp, which appeared to be acetylene. Three of the walls were covered with pictures and curtains but the fourth consisted entirely of windows.

Amelia said to Rodrigues in a tone that was half serious, half amused, "So it is you, after all! " He waved his hand by way of greeting and shouted: "The other girl is called Ginia, Guido". The soldier then shook hands with her, looking her over with an impudent smile on his face.

Ginia realised that the situation required self-possession on her part, and allowed her eyes to wander above Amelia's and Guido's heads to the pictures on the wall; they seemed to be mostly landscapes with plains and mountains but she also caught a glimpse of some portraits. The lamp that hung without a shade, such as one sees in incompleted houses, dazzled her without providing an adequate light. By looking hard, she could see that there were fewer curtains than at Barbetta's, though there was a red one which shut off the room at the back and Ginia concluded there must be another room beyond it.

Guido asked if they would care for a drink. A bottle and some glasses stood on the large table in the middle of the room. "We've come up to get warm", said Amelia. "We're drenched up to our knees". Guido poured out drinks — it was red wine — and Amelia took a glass over to Rodrigues, who left his recumbent position to sit up. While they were drinking, Amelia said to him, "If Guido doesn't object, I would be glad if, now that you're up, you would let me have the bed to warm up my legs in. Beds are for women. You come too, Ginia!" But Ginia did not wish to and said that the wine had warmed her up and sat down on a chair. Then Amelia removed her shoes and her jacket and threw herself under the bed-cover. Rodrigues remained sitting on the edge of the sofa as before.

"Go on with the conversation", said Amelia. "But this light's worrying me". She stretched out her arm up the wall and turned it out. "That's that. Give me a cigarette".

Ginia sat in the dark, terrified. But she realised that Guido had gone over to the sofa, heard him striking a match and saw the two faces in the flame and the darting shadow. Then darkness again, and for a few seconds no sound of breathing. You could just hear the rain dripping under the windows.

Someone broke the silence for a moment but Ginia who still felt ill at ease, did not catch the words. She noticed that Guido was smoking too and quietly pacing up and down in the dark. She could see the glow of his cigarette and hear his footsteps. She next became aware that Amelia and Rodrigues were having a tiff. It was only when she had gradually got used to the darkness and was beginning to distinguish the table, the shadow of the other people and even a few of the pictures on the wall that she felt less worried. Amelia was talking to Guido about an occasion when she had been ill and had slept on the sofa. "But you hadn't this friend in those days", she said, "eh, what are you doing, stripping?"

It was all so strange to Ginia that she said, "It's like being at the pictures".

"Except you don't have to pay for a ticket", remarked Rodrigues from his corner.

Guido was still walking up and down and seemed to be everywhere at once; the thin floor vibrated under his boots. They were all talking at once but Ginia suddenly noticed that Amelia was silent, though she saw the cigarette, and that Rodrigues was silent as well. There was only Guido's voice filling the room, explaining something, she could not make out what, because her ear was against the sofa. A light from the lamps outside came through the windows like a reflection from the rain and she could hear the rain splashing and pouring on to the roofs and guttering. Every time both the rain and the voices ceased, it somehow seemed colder. Then Ginia strained her eyes into the darkness trying to see Amelia's cigarette.

Now that it had stopped raining, they said goodbye at the door down in the street. Ginia was still seeing the studio, untidy, dripping with water, in the light of the lamp. Guido had relit it several times, to pour out drinks or to hunt for something and Amelia had shaded her eyes, shouting to him from the sofa to turn it off, and she had noticed too, Rodrigues curled up against the wall at Amelia's feet, motionless.

"Haven't those two got anyone to do the room for them?" Ginia had inquired on their way back home. Amelia had replied that Guido was too independent to leave the studio key with Rodrigues.

"Did Guido paint those pictures?"

"If I was in his shoes, I would be afraid that dago would sell them and sublet the room into the bargain!"

"Have you ever posed for Guido?"

As they walked along, Amelia told her how she had got to know Rodrigues in earlier days when she was sitting for some artist or other, and Rodrigues had turned up, as he had now, and sat down in the studio as if it were a café. He had squatted in a corner of the room and had looked from her to the picture without saying a word. Even in those days he had affected a white tie. He had behaved in a like manner with another model she knew.

"But doesn't he himself ever paint?"

"Who do you think would be rash enough to stand in front of him in the nude?"

Ginia would have liked to have another look at Guido's pictures because she knew that the colours would only be seen properly by daylight. If she could have been sure that Rodrigues was out, she would have taken her courage in both hands and gone there alone. She pictured herself going upstairs, knocking at the door and finding Guido in his soldier's trousers and laughing at him, to break the ice. The attractive thing about him as a painter was that he did not seem like a painter at all. Ginia remembered how he had held out his hand with an encouraging smile, and then his voice·in the dark room and his face when the light was turned up and he had looked at her as if they were a couple on their own, nothing to do with the others. But Guido would not be there now and she would have to cope with the other man.

Next day at the café she asked Amelia whether Guido would at any rate be off duty on Sunday. "A while back you could have asked me", said Amelia, "but I've not seen him for some time now". "Rodrigues has invited me to his studio whenever I care to go". "You want to look out! " said Amelia.

But for several days they did not see him at the café. "What do you bet he's expecting us to go and look him out, now that he has a bed available, just to create and to see us again? It would be just like him", said Amelia.

"It's a mess", said Ginia.

Thinking it over in her mind, she was convinced that Amelia's action of getting into bed and turning out the light in front of the others was not after all such a shame-faced business; Guido and Rodrigues had scarcely taken any notice of it. What worried her was the thought of what Amelia might have done on that bed in the old days when Guido had been the sole tenant.

"How old is Guido?" she asked.

"He used to be the same age as me".

But Rodrigues was not to be seen, and one morning while she was out shopping, Ginia passed down the street of that night. Looking up, she recognised the triangular façade of the studio. Without giving it much thought, she ran up the staircase — which seemed endless — but when she had got into the last corridor, she saw various doors and was unable to decide which was his. She realised that Guido couldn't be very important — there wasn't even a visiting card pinned on his door, and as she went down again, she thought sympathetically of him having to have the glaring lamp of that evening which must be a handicap as far as a painter was concerned. She made no reference to her visit next time she saw Amelia.

One day when they were chatting, she asked her why men became artists. "Because some people buy pictures", retorted Amelia. "Not all", said Ginia, "what about the pictures that nobody buys?"

"It's a matter of taste like any other job", said Amelia. "But they don't get much to eat".

"They paint because they get satisfaction out of it", said Ginia.

"Listen here, would you make yourself a dress if you weren't going to wear it? Rodrigues is the sly one: he gives himself out as a painter but nobody's ever seen a paint-brush in his hand!"

That day in point of fact he was at the café, drawing in a sketch-book with great concentration. "What are you drawing?" asked Amelia and took the book from him. Ginia had a glance, too, full of curiosity, but all she could see was an intricate network of lines which might have been a man's bronchial tubes. "What is it?

A lettuce?" asked Amelia. Rodrigues said neither yes nor no, and then they turned over the pages of the sketch-book, which was filled with drawings; some looked like skeletons of plants, some like faces without any eyes, only areas of black hatching, and others, you could not tell whether they were faces or landscapes.

"They are subjects seen at night by gaslight", said Amelia. Rodrigues laughed and Ginia felt embarrassed rather than irritated.

"Nothing worth looking at here", said Amelia, "if you made me look like that in a portrait, I'd cut you dead".

Rodrigues looked at her but said nothing.

"A good model is wasted on you", said Amelia. "Where the dickens do you find models?"

"I don't use models", said Rodrigues, "I've too great a respect for my materials".

At this point Ginia told him she would like to see Guido's pictures again. Rodrigues replaced his sketch-book in his pocket and replied, "At your service". The result was that they went along the first available Sunday and Ginia missed a part of mass to be in time. They had agreed to meet in the porch but Ginia found no one there and so she went upstairs alone. Once again she hesitated among the four doors of the corridor, could not decide which one it was, and descended half the staircase, then decided she was being stupid and went up again and stood listening in front of the last door. Meanwhile a woman emerged from another; she was unkempt and wearing a dressing-gown, she had a bucket in her hand. Ginia only just managed to get up to her in time to ask her where the painter lived. But the woman did not deign either to glance at her or reply and hurried off down the corridor. Ginia, flushed and trembling, held her breath until everything was quiet again and then hurried downstairs.

Every so often someone would enter or leave by the front door and look at her in passing. Ginia began to walk up and down, feeling desperate, especially as a butcher-boy was leaning against a doorpost at the other side of the street, leering at her most unpleasantly. She thought of inquiring where the studio was of the female concierge but now she might as well wait for Amelia. It was almost midday.

To make matters worse, she had not fixed any rendez-vous with Amelia and so she would have to stay on her own that afternoon. "Nothing seems to go right for me", she thought. Just then Rodrigues appeared in the doorway and beckoned to her. "Amelia is up there", he said casually, "and wants you to come up".

Ginia accompanied him upstairs in silence. It turned out to be the last door; it had been silent within. Amelia was sitting on the sofa, smoking as if she were at the café. "Why didn't you come up?" she asked suddenly in a quiet voice. Ginia told her not to be silly, but she and Rodrigues seemed so categorical that they expected her to find her way up that she found it impossible to argue and she could not even say that she had listened at the door — that would have made matters worse. But she had only to recall how quiet the two of them had been to realise that the sofa could tell a tale. "They take me for an idiot", she reflected, and tried to decide whether Amelia's hair was ruffled and read the expression in Rodrigues' eyes.

Amelia's hat — the one with the veil — had been flung down on the table. Rodrigues, standing with his

172

back to the window, was staring at her ironically. "Perhaps a veil would suit Ginia", remarked Amelia point-blank.

Ginia frowned and, from where she stood, began to survey the pictures above Amelia's head. But all those little paintings had lost interest for her. Lifting her nose, she could detect Amelia's perfume in the cold mustiness. She could not recollect the smell of the room from the last occasion.

Then she walked through the room, looking at the pictures on the walls. She inspected a landscape, then a plate of fruit; she stopped; she could not bring herself to look away; nobody spoke. There were some female portraits; she did not recognise the faces. She came to the back of the room and found herself before the high curtain made of some heavy material such as draped the walls. It occurred to her that Guido had collected the glasses from behind there and she said, "May I?" in an undertone, but neither of them heard because Rodrigues was saying something. Then Ginia parted the curtain to look, but all that met her eyes was an unmade bed and the sink-recess. Behind there too she could smell Amelia's perfume and she thought it must be pleasant to sleep alone tucked away in that corner.

SEVEN

"Rodrigues is dying for you to sit for him", remarked Ginia, on their way home.

"So what?"

"Didn't you notice how he was hopping round you, looking at your legs?"

173

"Let him! " said Amelia.

"Have you ever posed for Guido?"

"Never", said Amelia.

On their way across the piazza, they saw Rosa go by, arm in arm with someone who was not Pino. She was clinging to him as if she were lame, and Ginia said, "Look, they're afraid of losing each other! " "You can do anything on Sundays", said Amelia. "But surely not in the piazza. It makes you a laughing-stock". "All depends what you want", Amelia replied, "if you're silly enough and want to, you can do what you like".

Ginia had learnt from Rodrigues that Guido came and spent lots of his off-duty afternoons in the studio, painting. "He would paint in the night, if he could", Rodrigues had remarked. "A canvas in front of him is like a red rag to a bull. He has to go for it — and cover it! " And he had begun to laugh in his throaty voice.

Without saying a word to anyone, Ginia chose an afternoon when Rodrigues was at the café and went to the studio alone. This time again, her heart beat wildly as she went up — but for a different reason. She did not pause to reflect in front of the door which she found open. "Come in! " shouted Guido.

Ginia banged the door behind her in her embarrassment. She stopped breathless before Guido's gaze. Perhaps it was just an evening-effect, but the velvet curtain, catching a ray of sunlight, suffused the whole room with pink. Guido moved towards her, his head down, and said, "What do you want?"

"Don't you know me any longer?"

Guido was in his shirt sleeves as usual and in his grey-green trousers.

"What about your friend?" he said.

174

Then Ginia explained that she was on her own and Amelia was staying behind at the café. "Rodrigues told me I could come and see the pictures. We came one morning before but you weren't in".

"Sit down, then", said Guido, "I'm finishing something".

He went to a place near the window and began scraping a wooden board with a palette-knife. Ginia sat down on the sofa; it was so low, she felt she was falling off. His free-and-easy manner embarrassed her and a smile escaped her at the thought that all of them, painters and mechanics, were familiar like this from the start. But how pleasant it was, half-closing one's eyes in that soft light.

Guido made some remark about Amelia. "We are friends", replied Ginia, "but I work in a dressmaker's shop".

The light was beginning to fade in the room, and Ginia stood up and turned to look at a picture. It was the one depicting slices of melon which looked transparent and juicy. Ginia realised that the pink light in the picture was not just the reflection of the sunlight; it echoed the red of the velvet when she had first come in. She then understood that painters had to know about such things, but she did not dare mention it to Guido. He stole up behind her and looked at the pictures with her.

"Old stuff", he said at intervals.

"But they are lovely", said Ginia, with her heart in her mouth, because from one minute to the next she was expecting to feel a hand on her back. "They're lovely", she repeated, stepping to one side. Guido looked at the pictures but did not move.

175

While Guido was lighting his cigarette, Ginia, leaning against the table, began to ask him who were the subjects of the portraits and whether he had ever painted Amelia. "She's an artists' model", she added. But Guido suddenly came to earth and said it was news to him. "I've seen her sit", she went on. "I certainly did not know. Who's the artist?" "I don't know his name but she posed all right". "In the nude?" asked Guido. "Yes".

Then Guido began to laugh. "She's found her métier, then. She's always been fond of showing her legs. Are you a model too?" "No, I go to work", said Ginia sharply, "at a dressmaker's".

But she was slightly offended all the same that Guido had not suggested doing her portrait. If Barbetta had liked her profile, why shouldn't Guido?

"Amelia can tell lots of stories", she said, "she's up to all sorts of capers. I can't make out what her game is".

"It would be fun to get together, all of us, sometime", said Guido, "this studio has seen some goings-on in its time".

"It still does", said Ginia. "Amelia and Rodrigues did not waste much time".

Guido gave her a half-serious, half-mocking look. It was already getting dark and it was not easy to see his expression. Ginia waited for a reply that did not come. After a long silence Guido said, "I like you Ginetta. I like you because you don't smoke. All the girls who smoke seem to suffer from some complication or other . . .".

"There's none of that smell of varnish here that you get in other painters' studios", said Ginia.

Guido got up and began to slip on his jacket. "It's turps. A good smell". Ginia did not know how, but suddenly she saw him in front of her and felt a hand on the nape of her neck, and all she could do, like a fool, was open her eyes wide and bang her hip against the table. Red as a live coal, she heard Guido close to her, saying, "The scent you have under your arms is nicer than turpentine".

Ginia thrust him from her, found the door and bolted. She did not stop until she reached the tram. After supper she went to the cinema so as to take her mind off that afternoon, but the more she thought about it, the more she knew that she would go back. That was why she felt so much in despair. She knew she had been foolish in a way that a woman of her age should not be. She could only hope that Guido was offended and would not attempt to hug her again. She could have kicked herself, for when Guido had called out something to her from the top of the stairs, she had not listened to hear whether he was asking her to come back. The whole evening in the darkness of the cinema, she thought with a heavy heart that, whatever she might decide now, she would end by going back there. She knew that this longing to see him again and to ask his forgiveness and tell him she had been a fool would drive her mad.

Ginia did not go along next day but washed under her arms and scented herself all over. She was convinced that it was her fault if she had excited him, but sometimes she felt glad she had had the nerve because now she knew what made men amorous. "That's the sort of thing Amelia knows all about", she reflected, "but she must have gone pretty far in the process".

She found Amelia and Rodrigues at the café together. As soon as she had gone in, she was afraid they knew all about it, for Amelia gave her a look, but Ginia soon calmed down and affected to be tired and in a bad mood. She was thinking of Guido's voice all the time she was listening to Rodrigues trot out all the usual nonsense. Many things had now become clear to her; why, for example, Rodrigues bent over Amelia when he was talking to her, why Amelia closed her eyes like a cat, why Amelia seemed to be so thick with him. "He has all man's appetites", she thought, "he is worse than Guido, Amelia". And she could not help laughing as one laughs when one is alone.

Next day she went back to the studio. That morning at the dressmaker's, Signora Bice had drily remarked that they could stay at home that afternoon because of the *festa*. At home she had found Severino changing his shirt ready for the rally. It was a patriotic festival; banners were hung out and Ginia had asked him, "I wonder if the soldiers will have some leave of absence?" "I'd rather they let me have some sleep", remarked Severino. But Ginia, happy, had not waited either for Amelia or Rosa to pick her up and had gone off alone. Then when she was at the studio doorway she regretted she had not gone with Amelia.

"I'll go along for a minute and see if I can find Amelia", she said to herself and stole upstairs quietly. She did not really think that Amelia would be there because at that hour she knew she would be under the porticoes. But when she got to the door and paused to get her breath, she heard Rodrigues' voice.

178

EIGHT

The door was open and it was possible to see through to the skylight. Rodrigues' voice was loud and insistent. Ginia leaned forward and saw Guido propped up against the table, listening. "May I come in?" she whispered but they did not hear her. Guido in a grey-green shirt looked like a workman. His eyes were fixed on her but they did not seem to be seeing her. "I was looking for Amelia", said Ginia in a thin voice.

Rodrigues had stopped talking by this time and Ginia saw him on the sofa with one knee clasped between his hands, staring. "Isn't Amelia here?"

"This isn't the café! " said Rodrigues.

Ginia looked at Guido and hesitated. She saw him supporting himself against the table, his hands behind his back. His eyes narrowed. "We used not to have all these girls visiting us", he said, "is it you who attract them?"

Then Ginia lowered her head, but she could tell by his tone of voice that he was not angry. "Come in", they said, "don't be silly! "

That afternoon was the best Ginia had ever spent. Her sole fear was that Amelia should turn up and speak her mind. But the time went on, and Guido and Rodrigues kept arguing and every now and then Guido smiled and told her she ought to tell Rodrigues he was an idiot, too. The argument was about pictures, and Guido spoke excitedly and said that colours were colours, after all. Rodrigues, still clasping his knee, faltered and lapsed into silence sometimes, at others he cackled wickedly like a young cockerel. She could not follow Guido's theme but it was a pleasure to listen to

179

him whatever he had to say. He spoke with vehemence and as she gazed at him, she held her breath.

On the roofs, outside, the last rays of the sun were gilding the roof-tops and Ginia from her seat by the window, turned her eyes from the sky to the two men and saw behind in the background the red curtain, and thought how pleasant it would be to be snugly ensconced there, spying on someone who thought he was alone in the room. Just then Guido said, "It's cold. Is there any tea left?"

"There's tea and a kitchen stove. All that's missing is the cakes".

"Ginetta will prepare it today", said Guido, turning towards her. "The stove is behind the curtain".

"It would be a better idea if she went and bought the cakes", said Rodrigues.

"Nothing doing", replied Ginia, "It's your place to go, you're a man".

While the conversation continued, Ginia hunted for the spirit-stove, tea-cups and caddy behind the curtain. She put the water on to boil, rinsed out the cups in the sink there in the dark, curtained off space which the tiny flame did little to brighten. She could hear both their voices at her back; in that corner it was like being in an empty house surrounded by a great peace in which to collect her thoughts. She could only just make out the ruffled bed in that narrow passage between the wall and the curtain. Ginia pictured Amelia lying there.

When she came out, she noticed they were looking at her inquisitively. Ginia had removed her hat by this time, and having glanced behind her, picked up a large plate by the window, all daubed with colours like a palette. But Guido quickly noticed, looked among the

180

packing-cases and handed her a clean one. Ginia stood the cups, which were still damp, on it, returned to the stove and prepared the tea.

As they were drinking it, Guido told her that these cups were a present from a girl like her who had come to him to have her portrait painted. "And where is the portrait?" asked Ginia. "It was not a model", said Guido laughing. "Shall you be a soldier much longer?" Ginia said, as she calmly sipped her tea.

"To Rodrigues' regret I shall be free in a month's time", Guido replied. He then added, "You're not offended any more then?"

Ginia could hardly form her lips into a smile and shake her head quickly enough.

"Cut out the formalities in that case!" said Guido.

After supper, particularly, it was wonderful. Amelia, who called to take her home, was very happy too. "When there's a *festa* and people are idle", she said, "I'm always happy. Let's take a stroll and have a good laugh together like a couple of fools. Where have you been today?" she asked Ginia as they walked along. "Nowhere special", Ginia replied. "Shall we go to the hills and dance?" "No; summer's over now; it's too muddy up there". They seemed to find themselves on the way to the studio as if by magic. "I'm not going there", said Ginia, "I've had enough of your painters". "And who suggested we were going up there? We won't tie ourselves up this evening". They arrived at the bridge and stopped to admire the pattern of reflections in the water. "I've seen Barbetta; he asked me about you", remarked Amelia.

"Isn't he tired of drawing you?"

"I saw him at the café".

181

"Isn't he giving me the sketch-portraits?"

But while Amelia looked at her, Ginia was thinking about something altogether different.

"What were you doing last year when you used to go to Guido's?"

"What do you think? Having a good laugh and smashing up glasses".

"So you quarrelled then".

"Need you ask? One summer he went off into the country and no one had as much as a glimpse of him".

"How did you first get to know him?"

"Why should I remember? Am I an artist's model or not!"

But that evening it was impossible to quarrel and it was too cold to stand still by the water. Amelia had lit her cigarette and was smoking, leaning against the stone parapet.

"Do you smoke in the street as well?" asked Ginia.

"Is it any different from in the café?" retorted Amelia.

But they did not go and sit in a café because Amelia was already fed up with standing all day. They retraced their steps homewards instead, and stopped in front of the cinema. It was too late to go in. While they were examining the display of photographs outside, Severino emerged, looking sullen and annoyed. He raised his chin, acknowledging Amelia, then turned back and began to chat with them. Ginia had never known him so gallant. He at last gave his opinion of Amelia's veil and was amusing about the film. Amelia laughed but in a different way from when she laughed in the café if the waiters made some remark; this time it was with her lips parted, showing her teeth, as she used to when in company with her girl friends, but had not done now for some time past. Her voice was certainly hoarse; "it must be smoking that does it", thought Ginia. Severino accompanied them to the counter and paid for their coffees and told Amelia that they would have to plan a Sunday together. "Dancing?" "Rather!" "Ginia can come along too then", said Amelia. Ginia could not help laughing.

They went with Amelia as far as the door and when it was shut, they went back home. "Guido is about the same age as Severino", thought Ginia, "he could be my brother". "Life's a rum business", she reflected, "Guido, who doesn't know him, would take my arm and we would stop at the street-corners and he would tell me that I am a lady, and we would gaze at each other. To him I am Ginetta. We don't need to know each other to be friendly". And as she pondered, she trotted along by Severino, feeling as if she were still a child. Suddenly she asked him if he was fond of Amelia and realised she had taken him by surprise.

"What does she do in the daytime?" Severino replied. "She is a model".

Severino had not understood because he began to tell her that she wore her clothes well, and then Ginia changed the subject and asked him if it was midnight yet.

"You be careful", Severino warned her, "Amelia is pretty smart; you're just the stooge".

Ginia told him that they did not often meet and Severino said no more; then he lit a cigarette as he walked along, and they arrived at their door as if they were nothing to do with each other.

Ginia slept little that night; the bed-clothes seemed a

183

dead weight on her. But her mind ran on many things that became more and more fantastic as the time passed by. She imagined herself alone in the unmade bed in that corner of the studio, listening to Guido moving about on the other side of the curtain, living with him, kissing him and cooking for him. She had no idea where Guido had his meals when he was not in the army. Then she began to think that she had never thought of taking up with a soldier but that Guido would make a very handsome civilian, strong and with that blond hair of his; she tried to remember his voice which she had forgotten though she could recall Rodrigues' quite clearly. She must see him again if only to hear him speak. Then as she reflected, she found it difficult to understand why Amelia had fallen for Rodrigues and not for him. She was glad she did not know what Amelia and Guido had done together in the days when they smashed glasses. Just then the alarm went off; she was awake already, thinking of so many things in the warm cosiness of her bed. As dawn broke she regretted that it was now winter and you could not see the lovely colours that accompanied the sun. She wondered if Guido, who said that all colours were really one, was thinking the same thought. "How lovely", said Ginia to herself and got up.

NINE

Next day, at noon, Amelia called on her, but as Severino was having a meal with her, they only chatted generalities. When they were out in the street, Amelia told her that she had been to a woman-painter that morning who had given her some work. Why didn't she come too. This fool of an artist wanted to do a painting of two women embracing, so they could pose together. "Why couldn't she copy herself in the mirror?" replied Ginia. "Do you expect her to take her clothes off to paint?" retorted Amelia, laughing.

Ginia said she could not leave the shop any time she chose. "But this woman will pay us, you realise that?" said Amelia. "It's a picture that will take some time to do. If you don't come, she won't take me either".

"Won't you do alone?"

"There have got to be two women having a scrap, get it? There must be two. It is a large picture. We should only have to pose as if we were dancing together".

"But I don't want to pose", said Ginia.

"What are you frightened of? She is a woman too, you know".

"I don't want to".

They argued as far as the tram and Amelia asked her what she thought she had under her clothes to preserve like a holy of holies. She was in a temper and did not look at her. Ginia did not reply, but when Amelia told her that she would have agreed to take off her clothes for Barbetta, she laughed in her face. They parted on such bad terms that she was doubtful whether Amelia would ever forgive her. But Ginia who at first dismissed the matter with a shrug of her shoulders, suddenly panicked at the thought that Amelia might make her look a fool in front of Guido and Rodrigues, and she was not too confident that Guido would be ingenuous enough not to laugh at her as well. "I would not mind posing for him", she thought. But she knew very well that Amelia was a better figure than she was and that a painter would prefer her. Amelia was a fully developed woman.

At a late hour she called at the studio for a moment to forestall Amelia. It was the time when Guido said he always went along. She found the door locked. It occurred to her that Guido would be at the café with the other two. She passed by the café and looked in the window for a moment but she could only see Amelia sitting there, smoking, with her chin resting on her fist. "Poor blighter", she thought as she went back home.

After supper she saw from the street that there was a light in the studio and ran upstairs, overjoyed. But Guido was not in. Rodrigues opened the door and let her in and asked her to excuse him because he was terribly hungry and in the middle of a meal. He was standing up by the table, eating salame out of the wrapping; the light was as dim as on the previous occasion. He ate rapaciously, like a boy, digging his teeth into the bread, and if she had not been put off by his swarthy complexion and his shifty eyes, Ginia would have laughed at him. He asked her if she wanted any, but Ginia merely inquired about Guido.

"When he doesn't turn up, it means he's not allowed out", replied Rodrigues. "He'll be on duty at the barracks".

"Then I will be off", thought Ginia but dare not say so aloud because he was staring at her and would have realised that Guido was the sole reason for her visit. Undecided, she glanced round the room, which looked almost squalid in that depressing light, with old paper wrappings and cigarette-ends littering the floor, and she asked Rodrigues whether he was expecting anyone.

"Yes", said Rodrigues and stopped chewing.

Not even then could Ginia bring herself to go. She asked him if he had seen Amelia.

"You people do nothing but chase each other round", said Rodrigues, looking at her, "why, if you are both women?"

"Why?" repeated Ginia.

Rodrigues sighed. "Why? *You* should know. By intuition. Isn't that how women go on?"

Then Ginia writhed for a second, turning it off with, "Has Amelia been looking for me?" "More than that", said Rodrigues, "she wants you".

The curtain divided at the back of the studio and Amelia came rushing forward eagerly and Rodrigues, snatching a bite, scuttled round the table as if they were having a game of 'he'. Amelia had not got her hat on and though she seemed put out, stopped in the middle of the room and gave a laugh; but it was an unconvincing one. "We didn't know you were here", she said.

"Oh, you were having supper", said Ginia curtly.

"An intimate supper", said Rodrigues, "but it will be more intimate with the three of us".

"You were looking for Guido, I expect", said Amelia.

"I was just calling, but Rosa is waiting for me. I'm late already".

Amelia shouted, "Stop, little idiot!" but Ginia replied, "I'm not an idiot", and bolted down the stairs.

She thought she was alone when she turned the corner, but she heard someone running after her. It was Amelia, still hatless. "Why are you rushing off like this? Didn't you believe Rodrigues?"

Without stopping, Ginia shouted, "Leave me alone!"

She passed several days in this breathless state as if

187

she was still running away. Whenever she thought of those two in the studio, she clenched her fists. She dared not think of Guido and did not know how to set about seeing him. She was convinced she had lost him as well.

"I am a little idiot", she concluded, "why do I always run away? I still have to learn to be alone. If they want me, they can come and fetch me".

After that day she felt more at peace and thought of Guido without getting excited, and she began to take some notice of Severino, who whenever they asked him anything, dropped his head before replying and invariably disagreed with whoever had spoken; as often as not he did not reply at all. He was not such a fool, for all he was a man. She, on the other hand, had behaved like Rosa. No wonder people treated her like Rosa.

She gave up going to meet anyone at the cinema or at the dance-hall. She was content to walk in the streets all by herself and pay an occasional visit to the centre of the town. It was November and some evenings she took the tram, got down by the porticoes, strolled round for a short while and then returned home. She always cherished a hope of meeting Guido and glanced cursorily at every soldier as he went by. Chiefly out of curiosity she ventured as far as the café window on one occasion, her heart beating fast; she could vaguely see a number of people but Amelia was not among them.

The days passed by slowly but the cold helped to keep her indoors and Ginia reflected, in the middle of her depression, that there would never be such a summer again. "I was a different woman then", she thought. "Can I really have been so crazy? I've come through by a miracle". It seemed incredible to her that summer would come round another year. And she could

188

already see herself walking down the avenues in the evening, with sore eyes, going from home to work and back home again in the warm air, like a woman of thirty. The worst of it was that she had lost her former partiality for having her little siesta after lunch with the shutters closed. Even when she was busy in the kitchen she thought of the studio and she always had time to do some day-dreaming.

She realised afterwards that she had passed as much as a fortnight like this. She always hoped, on leaving the dressmaker's that she might have some surprise waiting at her door and the fact that no one ever turned up gave the sense of having wasted a day, of being already caught up in the following day or the day after that and of eternally waiting for something that never happened. "I am not yet seventeen", she thought, "I have plenty of time before me". But she could not make out why Amelia, who had run after her hatless, was no more to be seen. Perhaps she was merely afraid she would talk.

One afternoon Signora Bice told her she was wanted on the phone. "It's a woman with a voice like a man", she added. It was Amelia. "Listen Ginia, say that Severino is ill and come along to our place. Guido is here too. We will have supper together". "But what about Severino?" "Dash home and knock something up for him and then come here. We will expect you".

Ginia obeyed and ran home and told Severino she was having supper with Amelia; she tidied her hair. It was raining when she went out. "Amelia has the voice of a consumptive, poor wretch", she thought.

She had made up her mind to clear off if Guido was not there. She found Amelia and Rodrigues lighting a spirit stove in the semi-darkness. "Where's Guido", she asked. Amelia straightened herself and passing the back of her hand across her brow, pointed to the curtain. From behind it emerged Guido's head. He called out, "Hello!" and Ginia smiled at him. The table was an untidy mess of paper doylies and food. At that moment a circular reflection from the stove appeared on the ceiling. "Light the lamp", shouted Guido. "No, it is nice like this", said Amelia.

It was by no means warm and you needed to keep your overcoat on. Ginia went to the sink, drawing back the curtain and called out from there, "Whose birthday is it, this evening?" "Yours if you like", replied Guido softly, drying his hands. "Why haven't you been coming lately?" "I came and you weren't in", whispered Ginia, "Have you been confined to barracks?"

But Guido only smoothed her hair with his fingers.

Just then the light came on behind them and Ginia dropped the curtain and gazed at the still-life of the melon.

They waited until the space round them had got a little warmed up before they began the meal. Strolling about like this with her hands in her coat pocket was like being in the café. Rodrigues poured her out a drink and replenished the other glasses. "Don't begin", said Amelia. Rodrigues insisted they should. They carefully moved the table over to the sofa so as not to spill the contents of the glasses, and Ginia hurried across to sit next to Amelia on the sofa.

There was salame, fresh fruit, cakes and a couple of bottles of wine. Ginia wondered if this was the sort of party Amelia used to have with Guido, and when she had drunk a glass of wine, asked him point-blank, and

190

then the two of them proceeded to laugh and remind each other of all the funny things they had done behind there. Ginia listened jealously — she seemed to have been born too late and felt a fool. It occurred to her that artists are a joke because their lives are different from other people's; even Rodrigues, who did not paint, lapsed into silence and chewed away or, if he did air his views, did so in a jeering way. She took it all in, quietly hostile, angry because Guido had fooled round with Amelia.

"It is not very nice", she complained, "telling me all these things when I wasn't there".

"But you're here now", said Amelia, "enjoy yourself!"

Then Ginia felt a terrible desire to be all alone with Guido. Yet she knew that it was only Amelia's presence that was giving her the necessary courage. Otherwise she would have run off. "I don't seem to have learnt to keep quiet", she repeated to herself, "I ought not to get worked up".

Then the others lit their cigarettes and offered her one. Ginia did not really want it but Guido came and sat beside her and lit it for her, telling her not to inhale. The other two were engaged in an amorous tussle on a corner of the sofa.

Then Ginia leapt to her feet, pushed Guido's hands away, put down her cigarette and walked across the studio without speaking. She moved the curtain aside and stood still in the darkness. The conversation behind her sounded like a distant buzz. "Guido", she whispered, without looking round, and threw herself, face downwards, on the bed.

TEN

All four of them left the place in silence, Guido and Rodrigues accompanying them as far as the tram. Guido with his beret pulled over his eyes looked quite different, but he pressed her hands in his and said, "darling Ginetta". As they strolled along, the pavement seemed to be rocking under her feet. Amelia took her arm.

While they were waiting for the tram, they began talking about bicycles, but Guido came close to her and said in a gentle voice, "Mind you don't change your mind. I would never do your portrait if you did". Ginia smiled and took his hand.

When they had boarded the tram, Ginia stood staring at the driver's back and fell silent. "Go home and put yourself to bed", said Amelia, "it's the result of the wine more than anything else". "I'm not drunk", said Ginia, "don't you believe me?" "Would you like me to see you home?" said Amelia. "Leave me alone, for Heaven's sake". Then Amelia spoke to her about the other occasion, explaining how it had been, and Ginia just listened to the noise of the tram.

When she was alone, she began to feel better because there was no one looking at her. She sat on the edge of the bed and stayed there for an hour staring at the floor. Then she suddenly got undressed, flung herself down and put out the light.

The next day was sunny, and as Ginia got dressed she felt as if she had been ill. She thought that Guido would have been up three hours already, and she smiled into the mirror and threw herself a kiss. Then she went out before Severino should return.

It seemed futile walking along in the usual way, being

hungry, for her mind was fixed only on one thing, that from now on she must have Guido to herself without the other two. But Guido had invited her to the studio, he had not said a word about meeting her outside. "I need to be very fond of him", thought Ginia. "I'd feel let down otherwise". The summer had suddenly returned and with it the desire to go out, laugh and have a good time. She could not believe that what had happened was really true. She found herself laughing at the thought that in the dark Guido would have behaved in the same way if she had been Amelia. "It is obvious he likes the way I talk, look and how I am. He likes me as a sweetheart; he loves me. He did not believe I was seventeen, but he kissed my eyes; I am a grown-up woman now".

How pleasant it was to walk along all day, thinking of the studio and waiting for evening. "I am more than a model", said Ginia, "we are friends". She was sorry for Amelia because she did not understand the beauty in Guido's pictures. But at two o'clock when she came to pick her up, Ginia wanted to ask her something but did not know how to begin. She had not the nerve to ask Guido.

"Have you seen anyone?"

Amelia shrugged her shoulders.

"Yesterday when you put out the light, my head seemed to be going round. I think I cried out. Did you hear me?"

Amelia was listening attentively. "It wasn't me putting out the light", she replied gently, "all I noticed was that you had disappeared. I thought Guido must be murdering you. I hope you enjoyed yourselves at any rate".

Ginia frowned and looked straight in front of her.

193

They walked on to the next tram-stop.

"Do you like Rodrigues?" asked Ginia.

Amelia sighed and said, "Don't worry your head. I don't care for blond men. if anything I prefer blonde women".

Then Ginia's face softened into a smile and she said no more. She was quite happy to walk along with Amelia and feel they were on such friendly terms. They parted company under the porticoes, without fuss, and Ginia watched her from the corner where she stood, for a minute wondering whether she was going to pose at that woman-painter's.

Meantime she herself went back to the studio at seven o'clock and climbed up five floors without hurrying so as not to get red in the face. Without hurrying, but two steps at a time. All the while she thought that even if Guido was not in, it was not his fault. But the door was open. Guido had heard her walking along the corridor and had come to meet her. Ginia was now in her seventh heaven.

She wanted to talk and tell him all manner of things but Guido closed the door and the first thing he did was to hug her. A little daylight still fell from the windows, and Ginia buried her face on his shoulders. She could feel his warm flesh through his shirt. They sat down on the sofa without saying anything and Ginia began to weep. As she wept, she thought, "supposing Guido were to cry, too", and a burning sensation ran through her whole body as if she was going to faint. Suddenly the support was removed; she realised that Guido was getting up and she opened her eyes. Guido was standing there looking at her, puzzled. She stopped crying then because she felt as if she was crying in public. As he looked at her Ginia who could hardly see, felt more tears welling into her eyes. "Steady on", said Guido light-heartedly, "if there's so little to come into this world for, it's hardly worth crying over". "I am crying because I am so happy", said Ginia softly. "That's all right then", said Guido, "but let's know at once another time!" So that half-hour, when Ginia would have liked to ask him lots of things about Amelia, about himself, his pictures, what he did in the evenings and if he loved her, she could not screw up the necessary courage. She managed to get him to go behind the curtain, however; in the light she somehow felt in full view of everybody. While they were kissing there, Ginia quietly told him he had made her cry out yesterday, and Guido's manner then became more gentle; he cheered her up, renewed his caresses and whispered in her ear, "You see what's happening; I'm not hurting you, am I?" Then while they lay back in the cosy warmth, he explained all kinds of things to her, telling her he respected a girl of her sort and that she could trust him. Then Ginia squeezed his hand in the dark and kissed it.

Now she knew that Guido was so good, she became bolder and with her head leaning against his shoulder, told him she had always wanted to have him to herself because she felt fine with him but not with the others there. "In the evening Rodrigues comes back here to sleep", said Guido, "I can't put him out on the tiles. We work here you know!" But Ginia told him that she would be content with an hour, even a few minutes, that *she* worked too and had dashed away from the shop every evening at that time in the hope of finding him alone. "When you're in civilian life again, will you still see Rodrigues?" she asked him. "I should so like to see you paint when no one else is there". Then she told him she would sit for him, only if he would agree to that. As they lay stretched there in the darkness, Ginia did not notice that night was coming on.

That night Severino had to go to work on an empty stomach but it was not the first time, and he never complained. Ginia did not leave the studio until Rodrigues arrived.

Guido spent the last days before his demobilisation priming and drying his canvases, adjusting his easel and generally tidying the studio. He never went out. It seemed a foregone conclusion that Rodrigues would continue to live there with him. But Rodrigues always messed everything up and whenever Ginia was in hurry, started up a conversation. Ginia would have been only too happy to help Guido clean and tidy up the studio, but a glance at Rodrigues told her that it would have annoyed them, and she went back to go out with Amelia. They joined forces and went to the cinema because each of them was holding something back from the other and they would have found an evening's chat hard going.

It was clear that Amelia had something on her mind: she was railing against all blonds, male and female. But at the moment Ginia felt kindly disposed towards her and was unable to hide her thoughts. As they walked back home, she brought them out.

She asked her if she had come to any arrangement with the woman-artist. Amelia put on a puzzled look and told her she had let it go. "No", said Ginia, "what a thing to do; I know I've never sat but I'm sorry you have lost the job". "Don't mention it", said Amelia, "you've found love these last days, you can snap your

fingers at everyone else. Why not! — but if I were you,
I'd watch my step".

"Why?" asked Ginia.

"What has Severino got to say? Does he approve of
your friend?" said Amelia with a laugh.

"Why ought I to watch my step?" asked Ginia.

"You take away my best painter and then you ask?"

Then Ginia's heart began to thump and she felt
Amelia's eyes boring into her as she walked along.

"Have you ever posed for Guido?" she asked.

Amelia took her by the arm and said, "I was only
joking".

Then, after a pause, "No, it's much more pleasant for
us two who are women and know it, to go out for a
walk together than demean ourselves mixing with
unscrupulous oafs whose only idea about girls is to
make a bee-line for the first one they clap eyes on".

"But you go out with Rodrigues", said Ginia.

Amelia merely shrugged her shoulders and made an
exclamation of disgust, adding, "Tell me one thing, is
Guido careful, anyhow?"

"I don't know what you mean", said Ginia.

Amelia took her by the chin and forced her to stop.
"Look me in the face", she said. They were in the
shadow of a porch. Ginia offered no resistance because
it was all to do with Guido, and Amelia kissed her
swiftly on the lips.

ELEVEN

They walked on again and Ginia gave a frightened
smile under Amelia's stares. "Powder your face"', said

197

Amelia in quiet tones. Ginia, without stopping, looked at herself in her mirror until she reached the next lamp and did not dare leave off, examining her eyes and tidying her hair as well. "I may as well tell you — I have been drinking tonight", said Amelia when they had gone past the lamp-post. Ginia replaced her mirror and continued to walk on without replying. Their steps rang out on the pavement. When they reached the street-corner, Amelia hesitated. Ginia said, "Well, here we are". They turned and when they reached the door, Amelia said "Cheerio". "Cheerio", said Ginia, and continued on her way.

Next day Guido lit the light when she entered because there was a fog outside and it seemed to have found its way in through the huge windows. "Why don't you light the stove?" she asked him. "It is lit", said Guido, who was wearing his jacket this time, "don't worry, we'll light the fire this winter". Ginia walked round the room, raised a piece of material nailed to the wall and discovered a tiny room full of rubbish and piles of books. "What a nice room! Is this where you put your sitter?" "If it's in the nude", said Guido. Then they dragged a suitcase from under the bed behind the curtain; it contained Guido's wardrobe. "You've had models then?" asked Ginia. "Let's see the portfolios of drawings".

Guido took her by the arm. "What a lot you know about painters. Tell me, do you know any?" Ginia laughed, put her finger to her lips and struggled to get away. "Come on, show me the portfolios. You told Amelia lots of girls came here". "Naturally", said Guido, "it's my job". Then to hold her there, he kissed her. "Which artist do you know?"

"I don't know any", said Ginia, throwing her arms round him. "You are the only one I want to know and I don't want anyone else ever to come here". "We'd get bored", said Guido.

That evening Ginia wanted to sweep the room but there was no broom to do it and she had to content herself with remaking the bed behind the curtain, where it was as ill-kept as an animal's den. "Will you be sleeping here?" she asked. Guido said that he liked to be able to see the windows at night and would sleep on the sofa. "I won't make the bed then", said Ginia.

She arrived the following day carrying a parcel in her handbag. It was a tie for Guido. He took it laughingly and held it against his grey-green shirt. "It will look nice with your civvies", said Ginia. Then they went behind the curtain and lay on the unmade bed in each others' arms, drawing the coverlet over them because it was chilly. Guido told her that it was he who ought to be giving her presents and Ginia made a grimace and asked him for a broom to sweep out the studio.

The days when they had these brief times together were the best, but they could never have a leisurely chat because Rodrigues might turn up at any moment and Ginia did not want to be discovered with her shoes off. But one of the last of these evenings, Guido said he wanted to pay back his debts, and they arranged to go out after supper. "Let's go to the cinema", said Guido. "Why? let's have a walk instead, it is so nice just to be together". "But's it's cold", said Guido. "What about going to a café or a dance-hall". "I don't like dancing", said Guido.

So they met and Ginia felt impressed to be walking

199

next to a sergeant, then she thought it was Guido and no one else. Guido held her under the armpit as if she were a child. But he kept having to salute officers and then Ginia transferred herself to the other side and hung on to his arm. As they walked along like this, the street seemed somehow different.

"Supposing we meet Amelia", thought Ginia and began talking about Signora Bice, trying not to laugh. Guido was in a joking mood too and said, "In three days' time I shan't have to be saluting these monkeys. Look at their miserable shopkeepers' faces". "Amelia liked stopping to jeer at passers-by, too", said Ginia.

"Amelia goes a bit too far sometimes. Have you known her long then?"

"We're neighbours", said Ginia, "have you?"

Then Guido told her about the year when he had rented the studio and his student friends came to look him up, and there had been one who had become a monk. Amelia was not a professional model then, but she had been fond of taking her clothes off and they all used to gather morning and night and laughed and drank together while he tried to work He could not remember precisely when he had been with Amelia for the first time. Then one of their number had joined the army, another had passed his exams, one of them had got married: the happy days were over.

"Are you sorry?" asked Ginia, staring at him.

"Not as sorry as the monk, who writes to me now and again and asks me if I am working and whether I see anyone".

"But are they allowed to write?"

"They're not in prison, dammit", said Guido. "And he was the only one who liked my pictures. You should

200

have seen him; a strong chap like me, tall with eyes like a girl's. He'd got the hang of it; pity".

"I hope you won't become a monk, Guido".

"No danger of that".

"Rodrigues doesn't like your pictures; now *he* does look like a priest".

But Guido defended Rodrigues and told her he was an extraordinary painter — one of those who thinks deeply before he starts to work and never leaves anything to chance — and that colour was his only trouble. "There's too much colour in his country", he said. "He's had his bellyful of it as a kid and now he prefers to dispense with it. But, by Jove, he's clever".

"Will you let me watch when you paint?" asked Ginia, squeezing his arm.

"If I am still capable of painting when I get rid of this uniform. I used to get some work done before. I used to finish a picture a week. They were exciting, those days, but the good days are over'.

"Don't I matter to you?" asked Ginia.

Then Guido pressed her arm. "You're not the summer. You don't know what it is to paint a picture. I ought to fall in love with you to teach you all about it. Then I should be wasting time. An artist can only work, you know, if he has friends who understand what he's up to".

"Haven't you ever been in love?" asked Ginia, avoiding his eyes.

"What, with you folk? I haven't time".

When they were tired of walking, they adjourned to the café to continue their love-making. Guido lit a cigarette and listened as she chatted away to him, watching the people as they came in and out. Then, to please her, he drew her profile on the marble table-top. When they were alone for a minute Ginia said, "I'm glad you have never been in love before".

"I'm glad you're pleased", said Guido.

The evening ended on a rather gloomy note because it turned out that once Guido had said goodbye to the army, he intended going off into the country to see his mother. Ginia consoled herself as well as she could, getting him to talk about his parents and his home, his father's occupation and his boyhood days. She knew he had a sister called Luisa. But she was disappointed really that Guido was a countryman at heart. "As a boy I went about barefooted", he confessed with a smile, and then Ginia understood the reason for his strong hands and his loud voice and could not believe that a country peasant could paint pictures. The odd thing was that Guido should boast of it and when Ginia said to him, "But yet you stay here", he replied that the country was where real painting was done. "Yet you stay here", repeated Ginia. "But I am only really happy on the top of a hill", was Guido's reply.

From that moment Ginia, for some reason or other, thought frequently about Luisa and envied her her position as Guido's sister and tried to imagine the conversations which Guido might have had with her as a boy. Now she understood why Amelia had never tried to take up with him. "If he weren't a painter, he would just be an ordinary peasant"; and she pictured him as a conscript, one of the lads who go marching by with a handkerchief knotted round their throats, singing, and end up as soldiers. "But he is here", she reflected, "he's done his time as a student, and we both have the same coloured hair". She wondered if Luisa was blonde too.

That evening when Ginia had arrived home, she locked the door and then got undressed in front of the mirror and looked at herself, absorbed, comparing her skin with the colour of Guido's neck. Then she felt at ease again and it seemed strange to her that there were no marks left on her. She imagined herself posing before Guido, and she sat down on a chair in the way Amelia had done that day in Barbetta's studio. Heaven knew how many girls Guido had seen. The only one he had not really seen was herself, and Ginia's heart beat fast at the mere thought. How lovely it would be to become dark, slim, devil-may-care like Amelia all of a sudden. But she could not let herself be seen naked by Guido; they must get married first.

But Ginia knew he would never marry her, however fond she was of him. She had known this from that evening when she had offered herself to him. Guido was too good to stop his work to come behind the curtain with her. Only if she became his model could she go on seeing him. Otherwise one fine day he would find another.

Ginia felt chilly there before the mirror and flung her coat over her bare thighs; it gave her goose flesh. "Look, that's how it would be if I posed", she said, and envied Amelia who had ceased to have any sense of shame.

TWELVE

When Ginia had seen Guido the previous time, the evening before he went off to the country, she suddenly felt that making love in the way he wanted it, was a desperate business and she lay there as though benumbed, to such an extent that Guido drew back the curtain to see her face, but Ginia took hold of his hands to try and stop him. Then when Rodrigues arrived and Ginia left them to talk, she understood what it was not to be married and able to spend day and night together. She went downstairs, bewildered, and for the moment she was convinced that she had become somebody different and that they were all ignoring her. "That is why love-making is frowned on; that must be the reason". And she wondered whether Amelia and Rosa had called. Seeing her reflection in the shop-windows, reeling as if she was drunk, she felt she bore no relation to that vague image which was moving past like a shadow. She now realised why all actresses have that haggard look in their eyes. But it wasn't that that made you pregnant; actresses did not have babies.

As soon as Severino had gone out, Ginia closed the door and undressed in front of the mirror. She found herself unchanged; she could not believe it. She ran her hand over her skin as if it was something separate from her body which still gave a few final shudders. But she was otherwise no different; she was as white and pale as ever. "Guido should see me if he were here" she thought hastily, "I would let him look at me. I would tell him that I really am a woman now".

Sunday came along, and it was hard having to spend it without Guido there. Amelia came to look her out, and Ginia was pleased because she was no longer in awe of her, and having Guido to occupy her mind, she no longer needed to take her too seriously. She let her chatter away while she herself thought of her secret. Amelia, poor creature, was more alone than she was.

Not even Amelia knew where to suggest going. It was a short, chilly afternoon, damp with fog, which discouraged them from going to the sports ground to see the match. Amelia asked for a drink of coffee; her idea was to lie back on the sofa, talking. But Ginia put her hat on and said, "Let's go out; I want to go up to the hills".

Amelia, strangely enough, was quite submissive; she was feeling lazy that day. They took the tram to get there more quickly, though there was no particular hurry. Ginia discoursed, set the pace, chose the route as if she had a definite purpose. It started to drizzle as they began the ascent, and when Amelia grumbled, Ginia refused to show any concern. "It's only a mountain mist", she said, "it's nothing". They were now on the wide, empty road, passing under the trees of the park-enclosures; it was as though they were outside the world altogether, hearing only the gurgling of the roadside stream and the rattle of the trams in the remote distance. They began to inhale the freshly-washed air and became aware of the smell of rotting leaves, more pervasive than the cold. Amelia gradually came to life and they hurried along the asphalt arm in arm, laughing and saying they must be crazy and that not even lovers went to the hills in weather like that.

A luxurious-looking car came along, and, after passing them, slowed down. "We could have that!" remarked Amelia. A grey clad arm shot out of the car and beckoned to them. "May I offer you a lift?" said the driver when they were within range. He was sucking a caramel. "Shall we accept, Amelia?" whispered Ginia, smiling. "Rather", said Amelia, "he can take us as far as the Devil's House and then leave us to go on foot". As they walked on, he followed them at the same rate, making inane remarks and blowing his horn. "I am going to get in", said Amelia, "if you don't mind; it's better than wearing your shoes out". "Isn't your blonde friend coming?" the man remarked, getting out. He was in his forties and very thin.

They then got in, Amelia in the middle and Ginia crushed against the door. The lean man wormed his way under the steering-wheel and began by putting one arm round Amelia's shoulder. Seeing the dark, bony hand near her ear, Ginia thought, "If he lays a finger on me, I'll murder him". But they suddenly started off, and she had a side-view of a face, that bore an ugly scar on the temple, concentrated on the road. Ginia, her cheek pressed against the window, thought how pleasant it would be to spend her time travelling like this all the week Guido was away.

However, her dream came to an abrupt end. The car slowed down at an open space and stopped. The handsome trees had given way to this wilderness filled with mist and telegraph-wires. The hillside looked like a bare mountain. "Do you want to get out here?" said the man, still sucking his caramel, and turning to them.

Ginia said, "You go on to the café then, I'll walk back on foot". Amelia scowled at her. "She's crazy!" the man exclaimed. "I'll walk back", Ginia repeated. "There are two of you and two's company". "Stupid!" hissed Amelia as they were getting out of the car, "don't you see, it's not just talk with this chap; he'll pay". But Ginia turned her head and called out, "Thanks for everything. See you bring my friend home safely!"

When she got to the road, she listened a moment in the silence of the fog to hear if the engine had started up again. Then she laughed to herself and began the descent. "Oh, Guido, they're ruining me", she thought, and looked at the hillsides, sniffing the cold air and the country. Guido too was on the naked earth among his own hills. Perhaps he was at home near the fire, smoking a cigarette as he did in the studio to warm himself up. Then Ginia stopped as the picture rose before her of the warm, dark corner behind the curtain. "Oh Guido, come back!" she murmured, clenching her fists in her pockets.

She soon got back, but her soaked hair, splashed stockings and her weariness remained to keep her company. She threw off her shoes, stretched herself full length on the warm bed and communed in thought with the absent Guido. She thought of the smart car, sharing Amelia's thrill, and concluding that she must have met the gentleman before.

When Severino returned, she told him she was bored with working at the dressmaker's. "Have a change then", he said, unmoved, "but don't make me have to skip any more meals. Find some post with more reasonable hours".

"There's so many things to do".

"Mamma used to say you'd enough at home to keep you busy. Considering what you earn outside!"

Ginia leapt up from the sofa. "We've not paid a visit to the cemetery this year".

"I have been", stated Severino. "Don't lie. You know you haven't".

But Ginia was merely saying something for the sake of talking. Except for her small earnings, she would have nothing to put on her back and would never be able to afford gloves to put on for washing-up and so save her hands. And the scent, the hat, the face-cream, the presents for Guido would be for ever beyond her reach; she would be no better off than a factory-girl like Rosa. What she lacked was time. She needed work that could be disposed of in the mornings.

Moreover a job had its compensations. What would she have done during these days of Guido's absence if she had had to stay at home all day or vaguely wander round, worrying her head off? As it was, she went back to the shop next day, which she got through somehow. She hurried home and prepared a nice supper for Severino and decided to compensate during these next days for the meals that she had failed more than once to cook for him.

Amelia did not appear. Several evenings Ginia was on the point of going out when she remembered her private vow to stay in, and she hoped Amelia would call. Rosa came once. She wanted to make herself a coat and show her the pattern. But Ginia found it hard to make conversation. They discussed Pino, but Rosa did not confess that she had changed him for someone else. She complained instead that she was bored to death and said, "What do you expect? If you get married, you're landed".

Ginia realised that continually thinking about Guido was interfering with her sleep, and sometimes she got angry because he failed to understand that he ought to come back. "I wonder if he will be here by Monday", she thought, "I am sure he's not coming". She particularly hated Luisa, who was only his sister, and yet had the pleasure of seeing him all day long. She was overcome by such nostalgia that she considered going along to his studio and finding out from Rodrigues if Guido was keeping his word.

But she went to the café instead and saw Amelia. "How did it go on Sunday?" she asked. Amelia, who was smoking a cigarette, did not even smile, and said quietly, "It went fine". "Did he take you home?" "Yes indeed", said Amelia.

Then she asked, "Why did you run off?"

"Wasn't he offended?"

"What rot", said Amelia, staring at her. "All he said was: 'Spirited little piece'. Why *did* you run off?"

Ginia felt herself blush. "I thought he looked ridiculous with that caramel".

"You're a fool", said Amelia.

"What news of Rodrigues?"

"He is away at present".

They walked back home together and Amelia said to her, "Tonight I'll come and see you".

There was no talk of going out that evening. Ginia, having got the washing-up out of the way, sat down on the edge of the sofa, where Amelia was lying at full length. They remained thus for a while in silence, and then Amelia whispered in her husky voice, "Spirited little piece!" Ginia shook her head and looked away. Amelia stretched her arm out and stroked her hair. "Leave me alone", said Ginia.

With a great sigh, Amelia raised herself up on her elbow. "I dote on you", she said huskily. Ginia darted a look at her. "But I can't kiss you. I've got syphilis".

THIRTEEN

"Do you know what it is?"

Ginia's eyes expressed silent assent.

"But I didn't myself".

"Who told you, then?"

"Haven't you noticed how I talk?" said Amelia, in a choky voice.

"That's from smoking".

"That's what I thought", said Amelia, "But our fine friend of last Sunday was a doctor. Look! " She opened her blouse and showed one of her breasts. Ginia said, "I don't believe you".

Amelia raised her eyes, holding it between her fingers, and looked at her. "All right, kiss me here then! " she said quietly, "where it is inflamed". They stared at each other for a moment; then Ginia closed her eyes and bent forward over her breast.

"Oh no! " exclaimed Amelia, "I've already given you a kiss".

Ginia felt herself growing hot all over — she gave a stupid smile and blushed a fiery red. Amelia looked at her without saying a word. "I see you're a fool", she said finally, "you're being nice to me just now while you're in love with Guido and I don't matter to you any more".

Ginia was puzzled what to answer because she herself did not know what she should have done. But she did not mind Amelia's criticism, because she now knew what nudes and poses were and understood her jargon. She allowed Amelia to go on talking excitedly but at the same time she was conscious of a nausea like that she had felt as a child when she was having a bath and was undressing on a chair close to the stove

But when Amelia said that the disease was carried in the bloodstream, Ginia was frightened.

"What do they do?" she asked.

Amelia told her it was hopeless unless you took things quietly, and that they would take a specimen of blood from her arm with a syringe. She said they made them strip and kept them standing in the cold for more than half-an-hour. The doctor was always in a bad temper and threatened to pack her off to the hospital.

"He can't", said Ginia.

"What a kid you are!" said Amelia. "They could send me to prison if they had a mind to. You don't know what syphilis is".

"But where did you get it?"

Amelia looked at her evasively. "You get it love-making".

"But one of the two must have it first". "Quite", replied Amelia.

Then Ginia remembered about Guido and felt so faint she could not speak.

Amelia had sat down and was supporting her breast under her blouse with her hand. She stared round vaguely; in her present state, without her veil and in utter dejection, there was no wonder she was no longer herself. At intervals she clenched her teeth, baring her gums. Not even the perfume she had on could soothe her.

"You ought to have seen Rodrigues", she said all at once in her hoarse voice, "it was he who said you go blind and die of ulcers. He turned white right down to his neck". Amelia made a face as if she were spitting. "It always happens like that. He is all right".

Ginia asked her in such haste whether she was really certain that Amelia hesitated. "No, you've no need to worry; they've made a blood test on him. Are you afraid for Guido?"

211

Ginia forced a smile and lowered her eyes. Amelia kept quiet for what seemed an eternity, then she suddenly snapped out, "Guido has never touched me, don't worry!"

Then Ginia cheered up; so much so that she put her hand on Amelia's shoulder. Amelia frowned. "Aren't you afraid of touching me?" she said. "But we're not love-making", stammered Ginia.

Her heart did not cease pounding all the time Amelia was speaking of Guido. She told her that she had not even kissed Guido because one can't make love with everybody and, though she liked him, she could not understand why Ginia should find him attractive when they were both blonds. Ginia felt herself go hot all over again and was thoroughly happy.

"But if Rodrigues hasn't got it", she said, "it means you haven't either. They've made a mistake'.

Amelia looked at her rather shiftily. "What's your idea? Were you thinking he had given it to me?"

"I don't know", said Ginia.

"If he's afraid that a child ..." began Amelia between her teeth. "But not he. The Lord chasteneth. The woman who gave me the present is worse than me. She doesn't know it yet; it appears she may go blind".

"It's a woman then!" whispered Ginia.

"Has been for more than two months. This mark is a present from her", and she tapped her blouse. Ginia tried to console her all the evening but was careful not to come into close contact with her, and took comfort as she remembered they had never done more than go arm in arm, and that Amelia had said furthermore that you could not catch it unless you had an open wound because it was a blood-infection. Ginia was convinced, but she dare not express her thought, that these things followed in the wake of the kind of sins that Amelia committed. Then she tried not to think about it, for in that case they ought all of them to be sick people.

However, as they went downstairs, she told her she ought not to feel vindictive towards the woman in question; if she did not know, she could not be to blame. But Amelia stopped on the stair and interrupted, "Shall I send her a bouquet then?"

They made a rendezvous for the next day at the café and Ginia watched her walk off into the distance, deeply stirred.

Ginia could hardly bear with herself next day. She left the house an hour before the lamps were lit and hurried to the studio. She did not dare go up straight away because Rodrigues was asleep, and paced about in the cold underneath until she thought she heard him turn over in bed. Then she ran up, trembling all over, and knocked at the door.

She found Rodrigues in his pyjamas looking at her with sleepy eyes. After stalking round the room, he sat down on the edge of the bed. There was dirt everywhere, the light was as glaring as usual. Ginia began in a stammering voice and Rodrigues sat there scratching his legs until she asked him if he had been to the doctor's. Then they both let go about Amelia, and Ginia noticed there was a tremor in her voice. She averted her gaze from his ugly feet.

Rodrigues said, "I'm going back to bed; it's damn cold", and he went back, drawing the bed-cover round him.

When Ginia, still trembling, told him she had been kissed by Amelia, he began to laugh, lying there

213

propped up on his elbow in the semi-darkness. "We're colleagues then", he said. "Only a kiss?"

"Yes", said Ginia, "is there any danger?"

"What sort of kiss?"

Ginia did not understand. He explained what he meant and Ginia swore that it had been just a kiss between one girl and another.

"Innocent fun", remarked Rodrigues, "don't you worry".

Ginia was standing up in front of the curtain and on the table was a dirty glass and some orange-peel. "When does Guido come back?" she asked.

"Monday", said Rodrigues. "See that? It's a still-life". He pointed to the glass.

Ginia smiled and moved to the side. "Sit down, Ginia, here on the bed".

"I must run", she replied, "I've got to work".

But Rodrigues complained that she had woken him up and now she wouldn't even stay to exchange the time of day. "To celebrate our escape from danger", he added.

Ginia sat on the edge of the bed by the drawn curtain. "I'm worried about Amelia", she said. "Poor creature. She's desperate. Do you really go blind?"

"Of course not", said Rodrigues, "you get cured. They bore lots of holes in her and will remove some bits of skin and before long the doctor friend will be taking her to bed, you'll see".

Ginia tried not to smile and Rodrigues continued, "Did he take both of you up to the hills?" As he spoke he stroked her hands as if they had been a cat's back.

"What frozen hands", he said. "Why don't you come and warm them?"

Ginia allowed herself to be kissed on the neck, saying
"Be good!" Then she rose to her feet, blushing, and
dashed out.

FOURTEEN

That evening Rodrigues came to the café too and sat
down at the next table, over by Ginia.

"How's the voice?" he asked half joking.

Ginia was trying to comfort Amelia, explaining to her
how one got better, and sat there quiet and contented.
They hardly exchanged a glance with Rodrigues.

Amelia sat there quietly, too. She was thinking of
asking the time when Rodrigues said sarcastically,
"Bravo! so we're seducing minors now, are we?"

Amelia did not grasp the illusion at once and Ginia
quickly shut her eyes. By the time she had opened them,
she heard Amelia saying fiercely, "What has this idiot
been telling you?"

But Rodrigues spared her. He just said, "She came to
wake me up this morning to hear about you from me".

"He enjoys himself", said Amelia.

During the next days Ginia endeavoured to be on
her best behaviour because Guido was really coming
back, and she went to look up Rodrigues. Not at the
studio any longer; it was rather a frightening memory,
and, besides, Rodrigues was a long-sleeper, but at the
little restaurant where he ate and where Guido doubtless
went too. It was in the street on the tram-route and she
passed a few moments exchanging pleasantries and to
find out if there was anything new. She behaved rather
like Amelia and pulled his leg. But Rodrigues now knew

where he got off and no longer made passes at her. They arranged between them that she should go along to the studio on the Sunday and do a little cleaning-up ready for Guido's homecoming. "We syphilitics", said Rodrigues, "don't give a damn for anything!"

Amelia, however, had ceased going there. Ginia stayed with her on the Saturday afternoon and accompanied her to the doctor who was giving her the injections. They stopped at the door, and finally Amelia said, "Don't go up; they might find something wrong with you too", and ran up the stairs, with a final "Cheerio, Ginia", so that Ginia, who had started out quite cheerfully, went home depressed. Not even the thought that Guido would be there within twenty-four hours could comfort her.

Sunday, too, passed like a dream. Ginia remained in the studio all the afternoon, and swept round, polished and generally tidied the place. Rodrigues did not even attempt to get in her way. He even helped her to cart off mountains of waste-paper and fruit-peel. Then they banged the dust out of the books on the mantelpiece and put them on top of a bookcase. While they were in the middle of washing the paint-brushes, Ginia paused a moment, enraptured: the smell of the turps brought back the memory of Guido almost as if he was there. She smiled because Rodrigues could not understand.

"He's a lucky swine", said Rodrigues when Ginia had finished and was emerging from behind the curtain with a duster, "if he only knew it".

They then had tea together by the stove and looked through the drawings of Guido's they had found under the books; but Ginia was disappointed because they consisted only of landscapes and one portrait-head of an

216

old man. "Wait a minute", said Rodrigues, "I know what you're after".

And after a while came drawings of women. They looked like fashion-plates. Ginia was amused, for they were dressed in the fashion of two years before. Next came some female nudes; then male nudes, and Ginia hurriedly turned them over because Rodrigues, who had been leaning back against the wall, was now bending forward. Last of all came a drawing of a young woman, fully clothed; she had a squarish face and had the head and shoulders of a peasant. "Who is it?" asked Ginia.

"It'll be his sister".

"Luisa?"

"I don't know".

Ginia studied the large eyes and the subtle mouth. She saw no resemblance to anyone else. "She's beautiful", she said, "she's none of that dreamy look that you painters usually give them". "Speak for him", replied Rodrigues, "leave me out of it!"

Ginia was in such a happy frame of mind that, had Rodrigues known it, he might have kissed her, instead of which he lay back on the sofa looking depressed. If it had not been for a little daylight that still stole in through the window, Ginia could have imagined it to be Guido near her and would have caressed him. She shut her eyes to think of him.

"How nice it is here", she said aloud.

Then she asked Rodrigues once again if he knew the exact time of tomorrow's event and he said that Guido would certainly be cycling back. The conversation turned on the villages in Guido's part of the country, and although he had never been to any of them, Rodrigues jokingly described them as being composed

217

of pig-sties and hen-runs and with roads that were so rough at that season of the year that Guido might not be able to get away. Ginia pouted her lips and told him not to tease her.

They went out together and Rodrigues promised not to spill his cigarette-ash about. "I'll sleep on a bench tonight. How will that be?" They passed through the door smiling, and Ginia boarded the tram, thinking of Amelia and the girls depicted in the drawings, comparing herself with them. It seemed but yesterday that they had gone to the hills and now Guido was coming back.

She woke up next day in a great state of consternation. It was midday before she could turn round. She had agreed with Rodrigues that if Guido arrived, they would meet at the café. She went past it on tiptoe and caught sight of them at the bar through the window. Guido looked thin in his mackintosh; he was standing there with one foot supported on the metal bar. If he had been alone, Ginia would not have recognised him. His open mackintosh allowed her to see a grey tie; Guido in civilian clothes no donger seemed a young man.

He and Rodrigues were engaged in conversation and laughing. Ginia thought, "If only Amelia were there, I could pretend I was on my way to her place". Before she could bring herself to enter, she had to remind herself that she had tidied up the studio.

She was still hovering in the doorway when Guido spotted her. She walked towards him as if she was there by chance. Never before had Guido made her feel so ill at ease. Guido extended his hand to her in the midst of all the customers who were coming and going, and continued to speak with his head turned towards Rodrigues.

They hardly exchanged more than a word. Guido was nervous because of the others watching. He encouraged her with a smile, calling out, "Are you all right?" and then, by the door, "Good-bye! "

Ginia walked in the direction of the tram, smiling like an idiot. Suddenly she felt her arm taken and a voice, Guido's, whispered in her ear, "Ginetta".

They stopped and Ginia had tears in her eyes. "Where are you going?" he asked. "Home". "Without welcoming me?" and Guido squeezed her arm and fixed his eyes on her. "Oh Guido", said Ginia, "I was just waiting for you".

They went back on the pavement without speaking; then Guido said: "I'm going home now and when you come and see me I recommend you not to weep! "

"Tonight?"

"Tonight! "

That evening, before going out, Ginia did a special toilette in Guido's honour. She felt her legs give way as she thought of him. She went up the stairs in a state of panic. She listened at his door; there was a light but no sound of conversation. Then she coughed as she had on a previous occasion but nothing stirred within. She decided to knock.

FIFTEEN

Guido, smiling, opened it, and a girl's voice from the back of the room called out, "Who is it?" Guido offered his hand and asked her to come in.

In the half-light by the curtain a girl was slipping on

her mackintosh. She had no hat, and she looked Ginia up and down as if she owned the place.

"A colleague of mine". said Guido. "It's only Ginia".

The girl went to the window, biting her lips and inspecting herself in the dirty glass. She had the same kind of walk as Amelia. Ginia looked first at her and then at Guido.

"Well, Ginia?" said Guido.

The girl finally left but not before looking her up and down for a last time from the door. She slammed it and they heard her footsteps gradually die away.

"She's a model", said Guido.

That night they stayed on the sofa with the lamp lit, and Ginia no longer made any attempt to hide away. They had moved the stove up to the sofa edge, but it was still cold, and after Guido had looked at her for a moment, Ginia went back under the blanket. What thrilled her most as she lay stretched out beside him was that this was real love. Guido got up, still undressed, to get a drink and hopped back quickly out of the cold. They placed their glasses on the stove to warm them. Guido smelt of wine but Ginia preferred the warm smell of his flesh. His chest was covered with curly hairs which brushed against her cheeks, and when they threw back the covers, Ginia compared her skin with his and was abashed and contented at the same time. She whispered in his ear that looking at him made her feel shy and Guido replied that she did not need to look.

Only when they were locked in an embrace did they finally say anything about Amelia, and Ginia told him that a woman was responsible for it all. "She's brought it on herself", said Guido. "You can't fool around with these things".

"How you smell of wine", said Ginia in a low voice. "It's better than the smell of bed", retorted Guido, but Ginia stopped his mouth with her hand.

They then put the light out and lay quietly. Ginia stared up at the ceiling in a vague way and thought of so many things, while Guido lay breathing heavily at her side. Distant lights could be seen over by the windows. The smell of wine and warm breath conjured up Guido's landscapes. Then she wondered if her frail body was to Guido's liking and whether he would not prefer the slender, dark and handsome Amelia. Guido kissed her all over in silence.

Then she became conscious that Guido was asleep and felt they could not go sleeping like this, locked in each others' arms, and she disengaged herself gently and found a cool spot, then she felt uncomfortable, naked and alone. Again she was overcome with a kind of nausea, as when they bathed her as a child. She wondered why Guido made love to her and thought of the next day and all the days she had waited for, and her eyes filled with tears, and she wept quietly to herself so that no one could hear.

They got dressed in the dark and Ginia suddenly asked who the model had been.

"Just a poor devil who had learned of my return".

"She's good-looking, isn't she?" said Ginia.

"You saw her, didn't you! "

"But how can people pose in this cold".

"You girls don't feel it", said Guido, "you are made to be naked".

"I couldn't do it".

"But you have tonight! "

Guido looked at her; she could see him smiling.

"Happy?" he said. They sat side by side on the sofa and Ginia rested her head on his shoulder so as to avoid looking him in the eyes. "I am so afraid that you don't love me", she said.

Then they made some tea, and Guido sat and smoked a cigarette while she strolled round the room. "It seems to me I let you do what you like. I have even sent Rodrigues out for a walk the whole evening".

"Will he be back any moment now?" asked Ginia.

"He hasn't the door-key. I am going to take it down".

They parted at the door therefore because Ginia wanted to avoid seeing Rodrigues. She went back in the tram, feeling gloomy and without thinking about anything in particular.

She had embarked on her real life as a lover because she and Guido had now seen each other naked and everything seemed different. She felt as if they were married; even when she was alone, she had only to recall the expression in his eyes and her loneliness vanished. "Is this what being married is?" Had her mother been like this? She could not believe other people in the world had ever had the necessary courage. No woman, no girl, could have seen a naked man as she had seen Guido. Such a thing could not happen twice.

But Ginia was not a fool and knew that all of them said that. Even Rosa that time when she wanted to commit suicide. The only difference was that Rosa did her love-making in the fields and did not know the joy of chatting and being with Guido. Yet even in the fields it had been nice with Guido. Ginia's thoughts kept returning to those times. She cursed the snow and the cold weather which stopped them doing anything, and thought, numb with anticipation, of next summer when they would all go to the hills, have walks at night and have their windows wide open. Guido had said, "You ought to see me in the country. It is the only place where I can paint. No woman is as beautiful as a hill". Ginia was happy because Guido had not taken the model on and intended, instead, to make a picture which was to extend all round a room as if the wall was open and they would see hills and blue sky on every side. He had been working it out while he was in the army and now he messed about all day with strips of paper; he daubed them with his brush, but they were only try-outs. One day he said to Ginia. "I don't know you well enough to do your portrait. Let us wait for a bit".

Rodrigues was hardly ever to be seen. By the time Ginia came to the studio before supper, he had already gone out to the café. Others came instead to spend the evening with Guido — including women, because Ginia on one occasion saw a cigarette-end smeared with lipstick — then it was that in order to please him — she said she was afraid she was disturbing him, these people made her feel nervous. She suggested to Guido he should leave the door open when he was on his own and wished to see her. "I would always come, Guido", she said. "But I realise that you have your own life. I don't want you ever to find me a bore when we are alone". Saying things like that gave Ginia acute pleasure, comparable to the pleasure of being locked in his arms.

All the same, the first time she found the door closed, she was unable to resist the impulse to knock, feeling very tense.

Amelia sometimes came to her house after supper, wearing a worried look and her eyes sunken. They would go out immediately, for Ginia did not want her sitting on the bed, and they walked round the town until three o'clock in the morning. In her devil-may-care way Amelia would enter a bar and take a coffee, leaving traces of lipstick on the side of the cup. When Ginia told her that she might infect the cups, she replied. "They wash them, don't they", shrugging her shoulders. "After all, the world is full of people like me. The only difference is that they don't know".

"But you're a lot better", said Ginia, "your voice is not so husky".

"Do you think so?" replied Amelia.

They did not pursue the matter further and Ginia, who had so many things to ask her, did not dare. The only time she alluded to Rodrigues, Amelia looked black and said, "Take no notice of those two".

But one evening she arrived at the house and asked her, "Are you going to Guido's tonight?"

"I don't know", said Ginia, "he may have company".

"And are you going to let him get into this bad habit of not being disturbed? You stupid fool, if. you're as humble as this, you'll never get anywhere".

Ginia told her as they were on the way there that she thought she must have quarrelled with Rodrigues.

"He's as big a swine as ever", said Amelia. "Did he say that? And to think that I saved his skin for him!"

"No. He merely said that it is all an excuse you have faked up for making love with that doctor chap".

Amelia began to laugh grimly. When they had got as far as the studio porch, Ginia saw a light in the window above and felt desperate because up to that moment

224

she had been praying that Guido might be out. "There's no one there", she said. "Don't let's go up". But Amelia resolutely entered.

They found Guido and Rodrigues lighting the fire in the hearth. Amelia went in first, followed by Ginia, forcing a smile. "Well, look who is here! " said Guido.

SIXTEEN

Ginia asked if they were disturbing them and Guido darted an odd look which she could not interpret. Near the fire-place was a stack of wood. Amelia had gone over to the sofa and sat down, remarking quietly that it was cold. "It depends on your circulation", shouted Rodrigues from by the fire-place.

Ginia wondered whoever could be coming that evening, seeing they had even lit the fire. The wood had not been there the day before. No one spoke for a moment and she was ashamed of Amelia's offensive remark. When the wood had properly caught, Guido said to Rodrigues, without turning round, "Keep blowing". Amelia broke into a comic laugh and even Rodrigues' face lit up with pleasure. Then Guido got up and put out the light. The room, now filled with dancing shadows, looked quite different.

"We're always the same together, we lot", said Amelia from the sofa. "How cosy it is".

"We only need some roast chestnuts", said Guido. "The wine's here".

Then Ginia removed her hat, contented, and announced that the old woman at the corner sold roast chestnuts.

"It's Rodrigues' turn", said Amelia.

But Ginia quickly ran downstairs, only too pleased that they were not offended any more. She had to wander around for a while in the cold because the old woman was not there, and as she did so, she reflected that Amelia would not do what she was doing for anybody. She got back tired out. Among the darting shadows she could make out the figure of Rodrigues curled up back there by the sofa at Amelia's feet, Amelia was lying back; it was just as it had been on that other occasion. Guido was standing up, smoking and chatting away in the red glow.

They had already replenished their glasses and they were discussing pictures. Guido spoke of the hillside he wanted to paint: his idea was to treat the subject as if it was a woman lying extended with her breasts in the sun and he was going to give it the flavour and taste of women. Rodrigues said, "It's been done before. Change it. It's been done".

They went on to discuss whether in point of fact such a picture had been done before, at the same time eating their chestnuts and throwing the shells into the fire. Amelia threw hers on the floor. Then Guido held forth: "But no one has ever combined the two; I am going to take my woman and stretch her on the ground as if she was a hill against a neutral sky".

"A symbolic picture then. Paint the woman in that case without the hill", snapped Rodrigues.

Ginia had not gathered it at first, but it turned out that Amelia had offered to sit for Guido, and Guido had not refused.

"What, in this cold weather?" asked Ginia.

They ignored her remark, and proceeded to discuss

226

where the sofa should be placed so as to get both the daylight and the heat from the fire.

"But Amelia is ill", said Ginia.

"And what's wrong with me?" flashed Amelia. "My work won't involve moving around".

"It will be a moral picture", said Rodrigues, "it will be the most moral picture there ever was! "

They laughed and joked about it, and Amelia, who had refused all drinks so far, as a precaution, now asked for one and said it would be safe if the glass was rinsed out with soap and water. She said that was what they did at home, and described to Guido the treatment she was getting from the doctor and joked about the injections. She told him he need have no anxiety because her skin was quite healthy now. Ginia spitefully asked her if her breast was still inflamed. Amelia flew into a rage and retorted that she had got better breasts than hers. Guido chimed in, "Let's see! " They all exchanged glances and laughed. Amelia unbuttoned her blouse and loosened her brassière and displayed her breasts, supporting them in her hands. They had put the light on. Ginia looked quickly across but she could not face the malicious triumph that shone in Amelia's eyes.

"Now let's see yours", said Rodrigues.

But Ginia shook her head. She was suffering agonies. She looked on the ground to avoid Guido's gaze. Some seconds passed and Guido said nothing.

"Come on! " said Rodrigues. "Let's drink a toast to yours! "

Guido was still silent. Ginia suddenly turned towards the hearth, feeling that they thought her a fool.

So next day Ginia went to the shop, knowing that Amelia, in the nude, was alone with Guido. There were

227

moments when she felt she was dying. She had a picture of Guido's face staring at Amelia continually before her. She could only pray that Rodrigues was also present.

During the afternoon she managed to get away on the pretext of delivering a bill. She ran to the studio and found the door locked. She listened; there was no one there, apparently. Then she went downstairs in a calmer frame of mind.

At seven in the evening she found them all at the café. Guido was wearing the famous tie and was smartly dressed. Amelia was smoking as she listened. They asked Ginia to sit down as if it was a child they were addressing. They talked of old times and Amelia talked about her artist friends.

"And what are *you* going to tell us?" whispered Rodrigues.

Without even turning her head, Ginia said, "I'm a good girl".

They then went down to the arcades to stroll around for a while, and she asked Guido if they could meet after supper.

"Rodrigues will be there", said Guido. Ginia gave him a despairing look, and they arranged to meet outside for a few minutes.

It was snowing that night; Guido suggested going to the café for a glass of punch, which they drank at the counter. Ginia, shivering with cold, asked him how Amelia could bear to sit for him in such cold weather. "It is warm by the fireside", said Guido, "and she's used to it".

"I couldn't stand it", said Ginia.

"And who asked you to?"

"Oh, Guido", said Ginia, "why do you talk to me

like this? I only mentioned it because Amelia is ill".

Then they went out and Guido took her arm. They had snow on their mouths, eyes, everywhere. "Listen", said Guido, "I know all about it. I know you go in for these things too. There's no harm in it. All girls seem to like kissing each other. Live and let live".

"But Rodrigues . . ." Ginia began.

"No, you are all as bad as each other. If Rodrigues is the one you want to sit for, go ahead, come tomorrow. I don't expect you to account for everything you do in the day".

"But I've no desire to pose for Rodrigues".

They parted company under the porch and Ginia returned home in the snow, envying the blind who beg for alms and have ceased worrying themselves about anything.

Next day at ten o'clock she dashed into the studio. She informed Guido at the door that she had chucked her job.

"It's only Ginia", Guido shouted back into the room.

Snow could be seen on the roof-tops. Amelia was sitting on the couch in the nude. It had been placed lengthways before the lighted fire. She contracted her shoulders and implored her to shut the door.

"So you thought you'd come and keep an eye on us", said Guido, turning towards the easel. "Of which one of us are you jealous?"

Ginia sulkily approached the fire. She did not look at Amelia nor move over to Guido. Guido threw some more wood on the fire, which made the place hot enough for anyone to pose in the nude. As she went by, he slapped her playfully on the back of her neck with his open palm, and while Ginia was turning her head, he stroked Amelia's knee as if he were touching a flame. Amelia, who was lying on her back, rolled over to turn her hip towards the heat, waited until Guido had gone back to the window, then whispered huskily, "Have you come to see me?" "Has Rodrigues gone out?" Ginia asked in reply.

Guido shouted instructions from the window. "Raise your knee a little!"

Then Ginia plucked up the courage to turn round and looked at Amelia enviously as she moved away because of the intense heat. Guido, from where he stood at the easel, darted a rapid glance at both of them, which he immediately transferred to his sheet of paper.

Finally he said, "Get dressed, I've finished". Amelia sat up, pulling her coat over her shoulders. "Done!" she laughed. Ginia sidled up to the easel. Guido had drawn an outline of Amelia's body on a long strip of paper. Some of the lines were simple, others intricate. It was as if Amelia had become fluid and flowed on to the paper.

"Do you like it?" said Guido. Ginia nodded as she tried to recognise Amelia. Guido laughed at her.

Then Ginia, her heart beating fast, said, "Draw me too!"

Guido raised his eyes, "Would you like to pose?" he said. "In the nude?"

Ginia looked over in the direction of Amelia and said, "Yes".

"Did you hear that? Ginia wants to pose in the nude", shouted Guido.

Amelia laughed by way of reply. She started up and ran off towards the curtain, wrapping her coat round her as she went.

"You undress there, by the fire, I'm getting dressed here".

Ginia gave a last look at the snow on the roofs and murmured, "Shall I really?"

"Go ahead!" said Guido. "We are not strangers".

Ginia undressed near the fire, slowly but with her heart thumping so hard that she was shaking all over, and blessed Amelia for going off to dress elsewhere, so that she would not be looking at her. Guido snatched the sheet of paper off his board and pinned up another. Ginia put her things down on the sofa one by one. Guido came up and poked the fire. "Hurry", he said, "or I'll be using up too many logs!"

"Courage!" shouted Amelia from behind the curtain.

When Ginia was naked, Guido examined her slowly with his clear eyes. His expression was serious. He took her hand and flung a portion of the rug on to the floor. "Stand on that and look towards the fire", he instructed, "I am going to do you standing".

Ginia stared into the flames, wondering if Amelia had already gone out. She noticed that the heat was making her skin red and was scorching her. Now she could see the snow on the roofs without craning her neck round.

"Don't cover yourself with your hands. Raise them as if they were reaching up to a balcony", came Guido's voice.

SEVENTEEN

Ginia stared smiling into the fire. A shudder ran through her. She heard Amelia's light tread and saw her appear by Guido's side near the window; she was adjusting her belt. He smiled at her without turning round.

231

But she could hear another step close to the sofa. She was on the point of lowering her arms.

"Keep a natural pose", said Guido.

"How pale you are", remarked Amelia, "forget about us!"

At that moment Ginia grasped what was happening and was so frightened that she could not even turn round. Rodrigues had been there all the time behind the curtain and he was now in the middle of the room, looking at her. She imagined she could even feel his breath. She went on staring into the fire, and, like a fool, trembled all over. But she could not turn round.

There was a long pause. Guido was the only one who stirred. "I am cold", she whispered inaudibly.

"Turn round, take the jacket and chuck it over yourself", Guido said at length.

"Poor thing", said Amelia.

Ginia now turned round quickly and saw Rodrigues standing open-mouthed. She picked up her things and covered herself. Rodrigues with one knee bent forward on the couch, gasped like a fish, and smirked. "Not bad", he said in his normal voice.

While they were all laughing and trying to cheer her up, she ran barefoot to the curtain and desperately flung on her clothes. Nobody followed her. Ginia tore the waistband of her knickers in her hurry. Then she stood there in the semi-darkness; the sheets of the unmade bed nauseated her. They were all quiet outside.

"Ginia", said Amelia near the curtain, "may I come in?" Ginia clutched hold of the curtain and did not reply.

"Leave her alone", said Guido's voice, "she's a fool".

Ginia began to weep silently, clinging to the curtain.

232

She wept bitterly as she had that night when Guido slept. It seemed to her that she had never done anything else with Guido but weep. At intervals she stopped and said, "Why don't they go away?" She had left her shoes and stockings by the sofa.

She had been weeping some time and felt quite numb, when the curtain suddenly opened and Rodrigues handed her her shoes. Ginia took them without a word and only half saw his face and the studio behind him. She then realised how foolishly she had behaved, to be frightened like that. The others were no longer laughing now. She noticed that Rodrigues had stopped still in front of the curtain.

She suddenly was afraid that Guido would come and ridicule her unmercifully. She thought, "Guido is a peasant; he will treat me badly. What crime have I committed by not joining in the laughter". She slipped on her shoes and stockings.

She came out without looking at Rodrigues or any of them. She just saw Guido's head behind the easel and the snow on the roofs. Amelia rose from the couch, smiling. Ginia snatched up her coat from it, took her hat in her free hand, opened the door and ran out.

When she was alone in the snow, she still felt naked. All the streets were deserted; she did not know where to go. However little they had wanted her up there, they had not been surprised to see her at that hour. She found distraction in the thought that the summer she had hoped for would now never come, because she was alone and would never speak to anyone again; she would work all day and Signora Bice would be satisfied. It suddenly occurred to her that Rodrigues was not really to blame; he always slept on until midday and the others had woken him up; it was not surprising that he had looked. "If I had a figure like Amelia's, I would have taken them all aback. Instead of which I wept". Her tears returned at the mere recollection.

But Ginia could not despair utterly. She knew she had been foolish. All the morning she contemplated suicide, or thought that at least she had caught pneumonia. It would be their fault; they would be sorry later. But it was not worth committing suicide. She had wanted to behave like a fully grown woman and it had not come off. It would be like doing away with yourself for having dared to set foot in a luxury establishment. When one is a fool, one goes home. "I am just a poor girl in disgrace", she said to herself, walking close to the wall.

She felt cheered up that afternoon when Signora Bice called out as soon as she set eyes on her, "But what a life you young girls lead. You've got the look on your face like somebody who's going to have a baby". She told her that she had felt feverish that morning, glad at any rate that her suffering had been noticed. Returning home, however, she powdered herself up a bit on the stairs; she would feel ashamed in front of Severino.

That evening she sat waiting for Rosa, for Amelia, and finally for Rodrigues; she had decided to bang the door in the face of whoever called. No one came. In order to tease her, Severino threw a pair of socks full of holes on to the table, asking her if she wanted him to go about barefoot. "Whoever marries you will be in a fine mess", he said to her. "If mamma was here you would see". Ginia, smiling, her eyes still red with tears, replied that she would sooner die than get married. That evening she did not wash up. She stood at the door, waiting instead. Then she passed through into the kitchen,

234

avoiding the windows so as not to see the roofs white with snow. She came across some cigarettes in one of Severino's pockets and began to smoke one. She saw she could now cope with it: then she flung herself down on the couch, breathing hard almost as if she was ill, and decided she would smoke again tomorrow.

The relief Ginia felt at present because she no longer had to run round doing things infuriated her because she had learnt to do everything at high speed and she now had so much leisure on her hands in which to think. Smoking was not much help; her chief concern had been to be seen in the act and now not even Rosa came to look her out.

The worst time was the evening when Severino went out and Ginia waited on and on, always hoping one of the crowd would turn up and yet unable to bring herself to go out. On one occasion a shudder ran through her like a caress as she undressed to go to bed; she stood before the mirror and looked at herself confidently, raised her arms above her head and slowly pivoted round, her heart beating fast. "Supposing Guido should come in now, what would he say?" she wondered, knowing very well that Guido no longer gave her a thought. "We did not even say goodbye to each other", she murmured and dashed into bed so as not to burst out crying in her naked state.

Sometimes Ginia would stop in the streets as she suddenly became aware of the smells of summer, its sounds and colours and the shadows of the plane-trees. She thought of them while she was still surrounded by mud and snow; she would stop at the street-corners, desire catching at her throat. "It *must* come, the seasons never change", but it somehow seemed improbable now that she was all alone. "I'm an old woman, that's what it is. All the good days are over".

One evening when she was hurrying home, she met Amelia by her porch. It was a hasty meeting; they did not bother to greet each other properly, but Ginia stood still. Amelia with her veil was walking up and down expectantly.

"What are you doing?" "I am waiting for Rosa", said Amelia in a husky voice, and they looked at each other. Then Ginia frowned and dashed upstairs.

"What's the matter with you tonight?" asked Severino between mouthfuls. "Have they given you the go-by?"

When she was alone, Ginia began to fall into real despair. She was past tears. She paced round the room like one possessed. Then she flung herself on the sofa.

However, Amelia turned up later that evening. At first, as she opened the door, she could hardly believe it. But Amelia entered as if nothing was different and asked if Severino was in; then she sat down on the couch.

Ginia forgot all about smoking. They discussed what they were doing, really for something to say. Amelia threw her hat down and was sitting with her legs crossed; Ginia was leaning against the table by the lamp, which was turned low, and could not see her face. They talked about the terrible cold, and Amelia said, "I've had my share of it this morning".

"Are you still undergoing treatment?" asked Ginia.

"Why, do I look different?"

"I don't really know", said Ginia.

Amelia asked if she could have a cigarette; there was a packet on the table. "I smoke now, too". said Ginia.

236

While they were lighting up, Amelia said, "Is it all over then?"

Then Ginia blushed and did not reply. Amelia looked at her. "I thought as much", she remarked.

"Have you just been there?" stammered Ginia.

"What does it matter?" said Amelia, uncrossing her legs and jerking on to her feet. "What about going to the pictures?"

As they were finishing their cigarettes, Amelia laughed and said, "I have had a bit of luck with Rodrigues. He wanted to know if I loved him. Now Guido is jealous". And while Ginia forced a smile, she went on, "I am very bucked — I am going to be cured by spring. Your doctor friend said he took me in hand in time. Listen, Ginia, there's nothing particularly good on at the cinema".

"We can go where you like", said Ginia, "you lead the way"

Also published by Peter Owen

ALBERTA AND FREEDOM
Cora Sandel

978 0 7206 1263 9 • paperback • 256pp • £9.95
Translated from the Norwegian by Elizabeth Rokkan

'Ahead of her time . . . Like Virginia Woolf, though much tougher . . . A classic'
– *Times Literary Supplement*

'She has a sure poise and distance that has deserted today's novelist.'
– *Guardian*

'Excellently translated . . . the fascination lies in the picture, convincing, lively beautifully drawn, of the artists's Paris at the beginning of the 20th century.'
– *Glasgow Herald*

Alberta and Freedom is the second volume in Cora Sandel's acclaimed Alberta trilogy. Alberta Selmer escapes from her suffocating life in provincial Norway for bohemian Paris, its absinthe and endless talk of Cubism. But Paris is not all she imagined: although she begins to write small pieces for newspapers and periodicals, Alberta's self-esteem is low, and her inexperience makes her prey to the casual approaches of predatory men. Feeling her talent sufferand her freedom stagnate, Alberta faces a struggle to survive. After its publication in 1931, *Alberta and Freedom* immediately attained status as a classic and Alberta Selmer as one of the century's great anti-heroines.

www.peterowen.com

Peter Owen books can be purchased from:
Central Books, 99 Wallis Road, London E9 5LN, UK
Tel: +44 (0) 845 458 9911 Fax: + 44 (0) 845 458 9912